The Art of
Zombie Warfare

The Art of Zombie Warfare

HOW TO KICK ASS LIKE THE WALKING DEAD

Scott Kenemore

Illustrations by Adam Wallenta

Skyhorse Publishing

Skyhorse Publishing books may be purchased in bulk at special discounts
for sales promotion, corporate gifts, fund-raising, or educational purposes.
Special editions can also be created to specifications. For details, contact the
Special Sales Department, Skyhorse Publishing, 555 Eighth Avenue,
Suite 903, New York, NY 10018 or info@skyhorsepublishing.com.

www.skyhorsepublishing.com

10 9 8 7 6 5 4 3 2 1

Library of Congress Cataloging-in-Publication Data

Kenemore, Scott.
  The art of zombie warfare : how to kick ass like the walking dead / Scott
Kenemore.
     p. cm.
  ISBN 978-1-60239-956-3 (pbk. : alk. paper)
  1. Zombies--Humor. I. Title.
  PN6231.Z65K46 2010
  818'.602--dc22
                                    2010017582

Printed in Singapore

Contents

Introduction

This book is an instruction manual that will teach you how to fight and lead with the acumen, skill, and effectiveness of a **zombie.** It will teach you how to command actual zombies and how to command human soldiers you have trained to fight like zombies. You will learn to face your enemies—no matter how numerous and terrifying—with the unflinching stare of the undead. You will learn the qualities that make zombies effective warriors in any situation or battle scenario. And you will learn the strategies and tactics that allow armies to employ these tactics, on a massive scale, to decisively win campaigns and entire wars.

See, zombies bite. Zombies gouge. Zombies stick their flailing hands through barricaded doors and windows, randomly snatching for anything that looks remotely human.

A zombie's battle cry is usually just a guttural groan repeated again and again. (Sometimes zombies can manage entire words, like "brains," but even these are delivered more as an emotive declamation than as part of a declarative sentence.)

And yet what might at first appear to be a simplistic approach to combat (attacking everything they see on sight with no consideration for their own physical safety, etc.) emerges as an elegant strategy of economy when examined more closely.

Unlike today's modern warrior (or the knights of old) zombies require no equipment to do what they were put on a battle-field to do. Zombies come equipped, innately, with every-thing they need to fight. (While zombie films reliably contain lengthy montage sequences of humans "weaponing up" to fight zombies, in film after film, it is the zombies that triumph over the humans, who have fetishized their machine guns and RPG-launchers with an almost pornographic intensity.)

They say, "It is a poor craftsman who blames his tools." We're not here to talk about craftsmen (they're boring, and don't usually fight like zombies) but there's a point to be made nonetheless. Zombies don't use any tools—on the battlefield or otherwise—which gives them nothing to blame for their success or failure.

Zombies are determined fighters. Zombies have no "morale issues" in the trenches (or swamps, or dungeons, or shopping malls). They require no dramatically motivational speeches. Their resolve to fight cannot be influenced or demoralized by enemy propaganda.

Zombies inspire fear in whomever they attack. A zombie foe is unthinking, and this is part of its awesome fearsomeness. A zombie foe cannot be reasoned with. There will be no truce. There will be no sense that the battle isn't going well, and that really, the thing to do is to retreat.

When they fight, zombies fight to the end. They don't stop once the outcome of the battle looks to be determined. They don't stop when the enemy is dropping their flags, Gurkha knives, or M-16s and turning tail to run. Zombies only stop when your brain is in their stomachs.

If your goal is to be an unstoppable supersoldier, make a zombie your model, and you'll go far.

Let this transformation start from within.

The first part of this book, **How to Fight Like a Zombie**, establishes the many ways that military history has proven the zombie to be the apex of the contemporary soldier (or the soldier of any period, really). It will also focus on the skills that an individual would-be zombie warrior must adopt in order to succeed in close-combat situations. The traits that zombies use (and, as importantly, *don't* use) will be discussed to some degree, and the way that contemporary soldiers can cultivate these traits will also be examined.

The second part of this book, **How to Lead Like a Zombie,** will provide an introduction to the tactics and strategies that commanders on the battlefield can use to ensure their troops (however human they might be) engage their enemies in the manner of the undead. This section will also cover the fundamentals of raising a zombie army.

Okay, question time.

If you could design the ultimate supersoldier, what qualities would he have? Seriously. What skills and powers would the ultimate warrior (no, not the WWE one) need to exhibit on the battlefield in order to be considered the best possible example of what the military can produce? With which tactical, military, and general ass-kicking qualities would you imbue the ideal combat troop?

Would he be brave? Yes, of course. He would be the very picture of bravery. Stalwart always in the face of danger, the ultimate soldier would never retreat. He would never shrink from a task, no matter how steeply the odds appeared stacked against him. He wouldn't be able to spell the word *fear,* much less feel it.

Stamina? Of course. The ultimate soldier would willingly stalk through stinking, insect-infected marshes with never the impulse to complain. He would climb mountains, if that was where the mission took him, or explore ocean depths and bottomless sea trenches. He would walk across scorching deserts and frozen arctic wastelands if he knew it would bring him closer to the enemy.

Fatigue? It would not be an issue. This ideal soldier would toil ceaselessly to further your cause, never requiring R&R. (Instead of "rest and relaxation" zombies prefer "rending flesh and rotting.") Naps would be off the table entirely. The only breaks to be taken at all might be for chow.

Lethality? Now we're getting somewhere. Somewhere awesome. Your ideal soldier would live (or perhaps "live") to kill the enemy. It would be his one, all-consuming fixation, and he would have all the tools he needed to do it. His very teeth and talonlike hands would be as deadly as the most intricately designed firearm. When teamed with his compatriots in carnage, he would sweep across the land with the fury of an atomic blast or chemical cloud.

Defense? They say that the best offense is a good defense, but that's not really true in warfare. Really, the best offense is probably some sort of long-range laser that is also somehow a nuclear bomb. But considering that attacking people has a crazy way of making them want to attack you back, be sure to incorporate defenses into your ideal soldier. Armor plating?

Kevlar vests four inches thick? A zombie craves not these things. No, your ideal soldier would be naturally protected and require no armor plating. He would be able to absorb round after round of ammunition, if necessary, and have only the bare minimum of weak spots.

Discipline? A truly disciplined soldier would be almost prescient in his ability to adhere to the wishes of his commander. He would do what needed doing **all the time** and **without necessarily being ordered to.** He just would. He would find the enemy, and would then attack and kill them. Then he would do it again and again and again. He would be methodical and he would be ceaseless. Sound good to you?

Now that we have outlined the diverse qualities desired in your supersoldier, stand back for a moment and try to picture what he looks like, standing at attention before you. Is he an armor-plated knight from the days of yore? A bioengineered cyborg from some dystopian future (or first-person shooter)? Or is he, instead, a maggot-riddled, slack-jawed, stinking zombie, hardly able to stand at attention due to the constraints of his own decay?

Perhaps you hadn't considered that the walking dead would make the perfect modern soldier. Well, consider again.

Zombies provide not just one **but all** of the qualities one associates with superior soldiering. They are fierce, brave, loyal (after a manner of thinking), and are able to take and dish out damage with startling skill and acumen. They strike fear into the enemy unlucky enough to see them coming, and they inspire awe and respect in their human counterparts. Zombie armies have been able to sweep across entire countries and kingdoms, eliminating the human populace with the lethality of a weapon of mass destruction (while yet preserving all buildings, infrastructure, and indigenous wildlife). Zombies have advanced fearlessly into hailstorms of bullets and grenades.

> ### Do you want to live forever, maggots?
>
> Seriously, do you? Because if you do, then being a zombie soldier is actually a pretty awesome way to do it. You get to travel to exotic locations. You get to eat people's brains. Sure, there's probably an evil shaman or zombie-creating warlock telling you what to do most of the time, but still, it beats just sitting there in a coffin or something.

They have marched for months across the Earth's most inhospitable landscapes, with never a "this fucking sucks" to be heard. (However, they have been known to mumble ". . . braaaaainss. . . .") Finally, and perhaps most important, zombies have demonstrated time and again their collective ability to react appropriately in combat situations **with no prompting at all from a commanding officer.**

This much established, your mission should be clear.

If you want to "be all that you can be" as a soldier, then you need to "be like a rotting corpse on the search for brains" and use this book to turn yourself into a warrior, the likes of which the living world has never seen.

If you lust for the privilege and responsibility of military command—or just for the land and riches that can be taken with a zombie army—then use this book to raise an army of zombies (or, failing that, an army of human soldiers who have been trained to fight like zombies) and wreak havoc on the land with an awesome and indomitable army.

Have not a doubt in your soul; **nothing kicks ass on the battlefield like a zombie.** If you would succeed where Grant and Lee, Patton and Rommel, or Hector and Achilles have triumphed, then you need to make like Bub and Tarman. **And may your path to victory be marked with the brains of your enemies.**

PART I

How to Fight
Like a Zombie

Everything you know is wrong.

There, I said it.

When it comes to the art of warfare, your every conception could not be more off base.

Enemy surveillance, carefully coordinated attack plans involving feints and deception, long-range weapons . . . these are not the tools of a true warrior. These are lies. These are the tools of weaklings. Of failures.

The modern military-industrial complex seeks only to fatten itself by promulgating the untruth that expensive military equipment and years of strategy training at West Point are the most reliable tools for achieving victory on the battlefield.

I, on the other hand, am someone you can trust. I have no vested interest in deceiving you. I am here only to provide access to the laws that have allowed **zombies** to become the most effective fighting force in the world today.

You might shoot your enemies with M-16s, destroy them with fragmentation grenades, or send them through a skinless shrieking hell with a combination of napalm and white phosphorus. And that's, you know, fine . . . but notice also that you're not winning every battle you fight. You're not eliminating your enemy's entire army each time you engage it. You're not conquering the countryside with the swiftness and fatality of an implacable virus.

In short: **You are not fighting like a zombie, so there is room for improvement.**

Throughout history, the most brilliant military minds have sought to defeat armies of zombie soldiers. **All have failed.** No advance in their high-tech weaponry or cutting-edge training has ever allowed these leaders to match the tactics and fighting skills inherent in a bunch of stinking, rotted, walking corpses.

In the history of combat, there has been no foe as implacable and persistent as the zombie. Zombies have penetrated supposedly impregnable fortresses. They have forded uncrossable streams, traversed moats filled with flaming oil, and chewed through drawbridges on even the most impenetrable castles. They have risen from watery depths to overtake ships and sailing vessels—from ancient Roman barks to modern aircraft carriers—with ease and

> **Know guts, know glory.**
>
>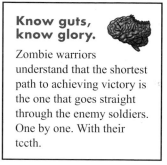
>
> Zombie warriors understand that the shortest path to achieving victory is the one that goes straight through the enemy soldiers. One by one. With their teeth.

facility. They have clogged the treads of tanks with their bones. They've attached themselves to helicopter skids (then hoisted themselves up to feast on the pilots inside). They've overtaken the most well-defended modern military outposts.

Zombies get close to their enemies and tear them limb from limb. Zombies bite off noses and ears. Zombies eat brains.

While zombies are often belittled, denigrated, and (most crucially) underestimated by their opponents, they always manage to somehow have the last laugh (or last brain). **It is this "somehow" that this section proposes to examine, quantify, and make available to the reader in practical, easy-to-understand steps.**

You need to ask yourself right now: "When it comes to zombies, do I want to beat them (clearly, an impossible task) **or do I want to join them?"**

Many soldiers wish that they could face their opponents with unflinching resolution, instead of doubt and anxiety. Many soldiers wish they were part of expeditionary forces that would operate autonomously and act with resolve, instead of requiring constant micromanagement. This section will make clear that these and other traits **can be adopted** by today's soldiers **if they copy the ways of zombies.**

Do you already have military training? Don't worry. It's nothing that can't be overcome. It's time to slough off the things you learned at West Point and replace them with things learned at Monroeville. Are you already a battle-hardened veteran? Prepare to learn more in three hours in an abandoned shopping mall than you did in three tours in the Middle East.

Let's be clear: **This is serious business.** The world needs effective soldiering, now more than ever. Today's geopolitical clusterfuck contains (but is by no means limited to):

- Traditionally warring ethnic factions
- Newly warring ethnic factions
- Tyrants and dictators who have ceased to be useful to the major world superpowers
- Insane religious leaders who encourage poor people to commit acts of violence
- Countries that are bored enough to fight over useless islands or horrible deserts in the middle of nowhere
- Third world paramilitary leaders who feel they'd do a much better job of running things than an elected president

All of whom will probably, at some point, need to have their shit set straight via a military engagement. These problems aren't going away, and it's important that a capable military is around to address them. **That "capable military" is going to be you.**

The soldiers of tomorrow are going to have a lot on their plate, and their ability to do what they do—effectively and efficiently—is going to be more important than ever before. Fighting like a zombie will allow you to achieve victory, destroy foes, and settle geopolitical conflicts with the quick decisiveness of a zombie's bite.

The world needs help from zombie soldiers, and if you're reading this book, then it looks like it's going to fall to you. Ask yourself if you're tough enough to get down like a member of the walking dead. If you are, then welcome to basic training.

Zombies Take It

The first thing to know is that **zombies are the perfect soldiers because they can withstand massive amounts of damage.**

Zombies can accept clip after clip of bullets into their chests or extremities and still keep going. Zombies can lose fingers, toes, or entire limbs without losing their killing capacity. They feel no pain when subjected to an enemy's weapons or the extremes of a harsh climate. Zombies can be cut, exploded, or set aflame, and still remain focused on the task at hand. Zombies will attempt difficult—or even suicidal—frontal assaults on your enemies without batting an eyelash (presuming they still have eyelashes). Zombies are easy to manage. Zombies clean up after themselves by eating any brains that have been left lying around after a battle.

A zombie will only stop fighting when its own brain has been damaged, when its head has become disconnected from the rest of its body, or if the zombie is somehow disintegrated.

An army of zombies is a fighting force that will be able to withstand—without complaint—enormous amounts of damage. Nothing touches a zombie when it comes to taking fire. Zombies understand that it is no excuse to fail to engage an enemy because they're "not wearing armor" or are "naked from the waist up."

A zombie will attack a human enemy under any condition, no matter how much injury it may have withstood personally. If it is not, itself, destroyed, it will attack.

If you want to fight like a zombie, you need to begin by thinking of ways to withstand massive amounts of damage. Are the other soldiers in your unit wearing flak jackets and helmets? Then maybe you need to think more along the lines of Batman-style Kevlar armor, or making your "uniform" one of those suits they wear to disarm bombs. Are you a medieval knight of some sort? You probably already have a nice advantage over the peasants around you, but make sure your armor is as reinforced as it possibly can be. Chainmail underneath the plate mail? Absolutely! You know, have fun with it. Get creative. Can you wear a giant helmet with full faceplate that has a smaller helmet with full faceplate beneath it? Then go for it, dude!

What's that? You say that unexploded bomb suits and "double suits of armor" make you move slowly and have trouble seeing? Hmmm. Who moves slowly again? Oh, that's right. **Zombies do.** And I shouldn't have to point out that many zombies' eyes are rotting away or are missing entirely. Count yourself lucky to be squinting out from beneath two visors, pal.

But here's the thing. All of this is a small price to pay for virtual unkillability. Sure, zombies generally move slowly and are half blind. Know what else? **They are the most feared entity on the battlefield.** When your enemies realize that none of the tools they brought to the dance are going to be any darn good against you, they'll start to realize just how much trouble they're in.

And that's when you get close and start dishing it out.

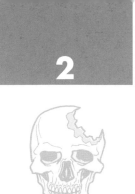

2

Zombies Dish It Out

If you're fighting zombies, then you're fucked. Let me say that again. Zombies. You. Fucked.

It's not complicated. It's not a concept that calls for eloquence, subtlcty, or language weaker than the word "fucked." When you fight zombies, you always lose. (If you fight **with** zombies, or **like** zombies, you always win.)

Zombies fight with their teeth and claws. Do not let their lack of firearms or melee weapons deceive you. If you dismiss a zombie as a threat because it isn't armed, then you're kind of missing the point. (And by kind of, I mean really. And by missing the point, I mean getting fucking eaten.) There is no limit on the damage a well-placed zombie can do.

Zombies fight without requiring ammunition. The importance of this cannot be overestimated. At the dawn of warfare, when the first cavemen started throwing rocks at other cavemen (just to be dicks, probably), humans encountered a problem that has stayed with soldiers to this very day: **the problem of ammunition.** Namely, that once you use it, it's gone. (So then you don't want to use it. But you need to use it. [That's the whole point of it.] But then, of course, it's gone, and so . . . Damn.)

Zombies have avoided the problem of ammunition by failing to use it (except in *very* unusual circumstances). This is not because they don't like it, but because they don't usually have it. Though zombies are few and far between, it would be remiss not to note that there are several extant examples of zombies being reanimated with guns in their hands (or, in the case of mad-scientist/evil-corporation reanimation scenarios, *attached* to their hands). And, in these cases, these zombies who found themselves holding guns **did** make use of them to attack humans. However, what's much less common—if it happens at all—is for zombies to seek out weapons to use against humans. The lesson is that zombies use whatever is at hand. (Or what is literally in their hands at the time.) This gives zombies important military advantages usually reserved for guerrilla warriors.

When zombies are attacking an improvised bunker in some kind of apocalyptic wasteland, each one will utilize different weapons as they become available. For most zombies, this is traditionally just claws and teeth, but some zombies may also have weapons with which to attack. Zombies don't worry about running out of ammunition. Why? Because even when its ammunition is exhausted, it's still a killer.

The zombie of a former soldier might find a firearm in some kind of underground military facility, and sure, it's going to kinda remember how to pull a trigger, and it'll probably take a few people out. But once the chamber is empty, it's not like the danger is gone. That zombie is still a brain-gnashing, barricade-busting, killing machine. It just doesn't have a gun anymore.

In some ways, a zombie is like a bomb or blind-fired RPG. It can enter an enemy position attacking indiscriminately. It doesn't matter if the humans it finds in that bunker are friend or foe, or if you just agreed to a cease-fire. Once the zombie is "on" (which is all the time), it's going to start killing people and feasting on their brains.

In other ways, zombies can be more precise than a tactical missile strike and provide the "light touch" so often needed in military situations. Is your enemy sitting on a warehouse full of valuable supplies? Sure, you can take his troops out with a long-range missile, but you'll also be destroying the very supplies you hope to capture. Flaming arrows, flamethrowers, and powder-based weapons all have the potential to create unwanted conflagration. But drop a few zombies on the warehouse roof (maybe send a couple down the chimney, if there is one), and you're going to dispatch all of your enemies while leaving the desired matériel intact.

As soldiers, zombies are a powerful tool because there is never a point (be it before, during, or after an engagement) when they are not dangerous. A zombie may be killed or destroyed, but it can never be disarmed. A zombie never surrenders or allows itself to be restrained. There are no zombie prisoners.

(**Note:** Zombies have been, in a few instances, imprisoned, yes. But this is only to say that they have been temporarily trapped, in, for example, a basement or a storage locker. But whereas a human POW waits to be liberated or to win his freedom through a prisoner exchange of some sort, an imprisoned zombie is searching constantly for a way to escape and never truly accepts its status as a "prisoner.")

Thus, a first step to managing your ammunition with the effectiveness of a zombie is not obsessing about running out. When you've got a clear shot, take it. Maybe you'll get resupplied, and maybe you won't. But that's shouldn't worry you, because **your ability to kill doesn't stop when you run out of bullets.**

If you want to dish it out like a zombie, **you must be prepared to attack your enemy at all**

When in doubt, attack!

Some soldiers are required to follow "attack plans" choreographed like synchronized swimming routines and/or wait for "orders" before jumping out of their cover and charging the enemy. Not zombies. A zombie never wonders if now might be a good time to attack. A zombie **knows** that now is a **great** time to attack, and it acts accordingly.

times, with whatever means are at your disposal. Does this mean that you should abandon conventional or long-range weapons and instead run, unarmed and slavering, toward your enemy while shouting "Brains!"? **No, it does not.** One thing zombies **never** do is cede an advantage to their enemy. If you're fighting with guns, concussion grenades, crossbow bolts, or whatever, **I'm not telling you not to use them.** (Zombies might very well employ long-range instruments of war, were they able to remember how they worked.) What I am telling you to do is to be **lethal at every range possible.** Carry your M-16, sure, but also maybe a machete or short sword; something that makes you deadly and doesn't have to be reloaded is essential for fighting like a zombie in short-range combat. Augment your martial arts training as well, in case you find yourself disarmed. If a zombie's tough enough to bite through skulls with just its teeth, you can darn straight learn a little karate or Tae Bo or whatever. Seriously.

Also, if you want to dish it out like a zombie, you need to cultivate within yourself the ability to fight tirelessly until an engagement is over. (A zombie never stops fighting, because a zombie is never "full." Its atavistic drive to consume human brains cannot be sated.) When a zombie is in the thick of combat, destroying its enemies and chowing down on their foreheads, it will repeat this activity until all humans present have been eaten. It doesn't matter if the zombie is shot, stabbed, or loses a limb. Though its powers of destruction may be lessened with each grenade or firebomb, a zombie understands that it has to keep pushing forward until all the salient work is done. When you go into battle like a zombie, you must continue to fight until all your enemies are dead. Being injured or running out of ammo is no excuse. No more bullets? Then grenades. Out of grenades? Then the bowie knife. Knife breaks or is lost? Hand-to-fucking-hand. Do you see where I'm going with this?

When you are completely committed to dishing it out like a member of the walking dead—with whatever means are necessary and until all your foes are dead—you will reap the benefits enjoyed by a zombie warrior. Your enemies will tremble in terror of your approach, for they'll understand that "once it's on, it's on," and that no amount of white flags, cries of "We surrender," or intercessions from UN peacekeepers can stop the carnage you're prepared to bring. They'll know that even when your gun ceases to fire, and your weapons supply has dwindled to nothing, they still are not safe. Your enemy will recognize that you have the ability to kill them with just your hands and teeth, and they will tremble before you as though you **were** a zombie.

If You Can Do It,
You Can Do It

Kicking ass like a zombie is as much about what you *don't* do as it is about what you do. And one important thing that zombies don't do—ever—is obey conventions, treaties, or rules of any kind governing their behavior on the battlefield. No zombie has ever agreed not to eat the brains of women and children, or not to eat the brains of prisoners of war, or to refrain from using certain tactics on the battlefield. Zombies do not allow themselves to be bound by documents or contracts, and so find themselves unfettered killing machines with infinite options when it comes to *kicking your ass.*

(**Note:** The source of zombies' reluctance to honor the conventions of war is not explicitly known, but it probably derives from the alacrity of **their own enemies** to use **any and all** means of warfare available to kill the undead. Zombies have

been shot, stabbed, exploded, gassed, exposed to radiation, poisoned, and set on fire. [Not all of these are effective against zombies, but you can't blame people for trying.] Nuclear strikes have been ordered against cities containing zombies. Scientists have captured zombies and subjected them to every harsh scientific compound known to man [with, again, often negligible effect]. The point is that if humans are going to have zero compunction about using the most horrible, lethal weapons possible when fighting zombies, then what sense would it make for zombies to have compunction when it came to their own fighting tactics?)

Compared to a zombie, a typical conventional soldier is weak, because he is confronted daily with battlefield scenarios that force him to hesitate and ask, "Wait, can I **do** that?"

Whether it's using chemical weapons in population centers, firing on unarmed protesters, or eating the brains of captured civilians, typical soldiers are constantly forced to second-guess their own actions on and off the battlefield. After all, soldiers who defy the rules of war can face courts-martial, and commanders who break the rules can face extradition to the Hague or worse.

Zombie soldiers never consider themselves bound by the jurisdiction of treaties signed years ago by a bunch of people who thought they'd fought "the war to end all wars" anyway. (Dumbasses.) For a zombie, the battlefield credo is only this:

"If you can do it, you can do it."

To put it more descriptively (though perhaps less memorably): "If what you propose to do is physically possible, then nothing prevents you from completing that action." Being bound by nothing other than the laws of physics, a zombie has only to consider forces such as gravity and inertia when preparing to dispatch its enemies in the most ghoulish and violent way possible. While regular soldiers hesitate to pull the trigger because of what a UN Special Envoy on Human Rights Abuses might say, a zombie eats the brains of everyone all around it all the time and **never** worries about persons or entities becoming upset by its actions. This innovation allows zombies to act decisively in crucial battlefield situations that might leave ordinary soldiers uneasy, hesitant, and ultimately ineffective. Allow the following hypothetical scenarios to illustrate this very real point.

Scenario: The enemy has embedded itself in a small hillside village in a craggy, mountainous region. There may, however, be indigenous residents also residing in the village—sympathizers, to be sure, but not enemy soldiers, strictly speaking. The approach to this village would leave your squad exposed and vulnerable. Once you reached it, you would have the dangerous task of going house-to-house and flushing out the enemy.

Typical soldier: "All right, so obviously we can't just call in an air strike and have them blow the entire hillside to smithereens . . . but we **could** radio the corps of engineers and have them come in and just dynamite the entire hillside. The ensuing rock slide would destroy the village completely, along with any insurgents hiding there. And maybe we could just say it was a natural disaster, right? I mean, rock slides happen all the time out here. But then again, somebody's likely to squeal at some point, and then whose ass is it going to be?" *Meanwhile, insurgents have escaped to a different mountain village, so even if you do move on it, now it's the wrong one.*

Zombie soldier: *Attacks the village, killing/consuming all enemy soldiers and anybody else stupid enough to be in the area. Historically significant mountain geography and natural scenic rock slides are left thoughtfully preserved.*

Scenario: In the course of liberating a small Central American country from its democratically elected leaders, your squad is confronted by a group of well-to-do-looking, upper-class-accent-having refugees who claim to be politically connected throughout the country. These refugees make the case that they could be useful to your side once order is restored by helping to promulgate your new political ethos across the country and also making sure you collect tax revenue from all of the local industrial kingpins who might be holding out on you. Your orders, however, are to shoot everyone on sight who has not already surrendered.

Typical soldier: "Obviously, this poses a problem. Maybe these guys are just talking a big game so we won't, you know, kill them, and they actually wouldn't really be useful to us. But at the same time, if they really would have come in handy—and we do execute them—then our commanding officer (or whoever's in charge of this junta . . . I forget) is going to be really, really pissed. . . . Fuck, this is a tough one. . . ." *While you're standing there, trying to decide what to do about this, government loyalist soldiers leap out from the shadows and ambush you before you knew what happened.*

Zombie soldier: *Refugees instantly killed/eaten. Moral quandary and ambush avoided.*

Scenario: This enemy-held airport is proving more difficult to take than you anticipated.

Typical soldier: "So there's this stuff called white phosphorus that is *totally awesome* to use on the enemy—you shoot some of it at them, and then there's this blinding white light and they're instantly burned up where they stand in this really horrible way. But because it's **so** horrible to be killed by white phosphorus, there are all of these stupid 'international treaties' forbidding the indiscriminate blind-firing of white phosphorus at nonspecific targets. Something about the chances of killing civilians in the most horrible way possible, or something. . . . But anyhow, in addition to making people burst into flame, white phosphorus creates an incredibly bright glow that lasts a long time. Thus, it **is** approved for battlefield use **for the purpose of illumination only**, presumably so that you can see your enemy and then kill them with conventional rounds. So what if . . . what if . . . stay with me here . . . what if we were going to shoot the white phosphorous *next to* the airport to light it up, so we could then see the enemy and pick them off one by one . . . but we 'miss' and 'accidentally' hit the airport itself with the white phosphorous. Then all of the bad guys go up in flames. Battle over. We win. But then again, that CNN camera crew is just up the road a couple of miles. But what the hell, right? So what if they get a little footage? What's the worst thing that could happen? Oh wait, really? 'Cause that's horrible. Maybe we need to sit here and rethink this while we get picked off by snipers. . . ."

Zombie soldier: *Attacks airport instantly with all means at its disposal. (This could include white phosphorus or just good old teeth and fingernails.) Enemies killed. Supply planes cleared for landing.*

In situation after situation, zombies address whatever problem confronts them with directness that does not find itself impeded by the "consequences" of how an external audience might view their actions. So if you want to fight like a zombie, remember that sticky situations call for only one question: "Can I do it?" Because if you can, **then you can.** Zombies didn't get where they are today by wondering if it would be "all right" with people if they stormed through a shopping mall consuming all the consumers, or if it would be "within the bounds of the Geneva Convention" if they ate all the citizens of Geneva.

When you see a zombie contemplating a stranded school bus full of children or surveying an arriving boatload of delicious immigrants (conveniently packed in like sardines), remember: It's never thinking, "Is this okay for me to do?" Instead, it's thinking, "Can I do this?" And if it can, then it does.

And so must you.

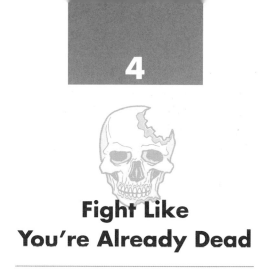

Fight Like
You're Already Dead

It's a simple idea, really, but one that can have a massively positive impact on your ability to do your job on the modern battlefield.

Fighting like they're dead is something zombies do because they **actually are dead.** (The word "like" hardly needs to be applied, really.) Being dead brings with it several advantages, however, that often give zombies the edge they need in combat situations. Chief among these is an almost total and complete lack of fear.

Most soldiers on the battlefield have—if we're honest about it—two priorities:

- Accomplish mission (e.g., kill enemies, blow up supply bunker, assassinate Saddam/Hitler/Osama)
- Not die

And they aren't necessarily prioritized in that order. Usually, for one to happen, the other has to happen, too. But when it comes right down to it and a soldier has to choose one, what are the things that would make him or her choose to accomplish the mission **even if doing so would mean his death?**

The answer is: the notion that death is a certainty.

If you're going to be KIA no matter what, you might as well try to get the job done, whatever it is. I mean, what else are you gonna do? Just sit there and wait around to get killed? Hell no. If you're going down, at the very least you want to take a few of the bad guys with you.

The trick is gaining the sense that death is inevitable. To make the point clear, let's start with a less extreme example. Like jogging.

Let's say you've let yourself go for a few years, but now you want to get back in shape, so you decide to start jogging again. But with your flabby gut

I regret that I have but many, many zombie "lives" to give to my country.

How many times can you reanimate a blasted-apart zombie and get it back into fighting shape? I dunno, but let's find out!

and man-boobs, you feel a little self-conscious about getting back out there. It'll be embarrassing. You'll be "the fat guy" in the park or on the treadmill at the health club. So, consequently, you start to put it off more and more. You find excuses not to go. You procrastinate. **Maybe you fail to go jogging at all.**

Why? Because you're afraid you'll be embarrassed as "the fat guy."

What's the solution? (No, not "work out at home" or "jog at night.") Don't **take the risk** that you **might** be embarrassed. Instead, **ensure that you'll be embarrassed.**

Make yourself a Day-Glo T-shirt with lettering that reads: "Get a load of my ginormous man-boobs!" Compose a route for your jog that takes you past the homes of all your ex-lovers and former business partners who are now more successful and thinner than you. Wear jogging shorts that are far too tight and expose parts of your backside that should never, ever be seen. You've got to make it more than a daily jog. You've got to make it a daily-jog-and-exercise-in-total-humiliation. You can be like: "Honey, I'm going out for my daily-jog-and-exercise-in-total-humiliation. Time to get my heart rate up while bawling like a little girl at my own shame! Be back soon!"

When the fact that something **might** occur is dissuading you from taking an action you need to take, you need to **ensure** that it occurs and, in doing so, give your fears no place to go.

Anyhow, let's leave the fat jogger and go back to the battlefield. Obviously, you don't want to ensure that you die—like shoot yourself or something—but you need to be ready for that possibility. (This is war, after all.) Just as our self-conscious jogger has to stop thinking, "I could be embarrassed if I do that," a soldier who truly wants to fight like a zombie must never allow the phrase "I could get killed if I do that" to prevent him from acting.

Zombies can of course be "killed" (or "killed again" or "rendered still") by disconnecting their heads from the rest of their bodies, or by penetrating or destroying their brains. Zombies do not walk with a swagger because they are invulnerable. Rather, they take the battlefield with the confidence of one well prepared for the eventuality of death. (Also, they've died once already and probably have the sense that it's not all that bad.)

To be clear, zombies never **try** to kill themselves. They don't leap into lava pits, position themselves in front of artillery cannons, or turn melee weapons on themselves. (There is no record, anywhere, of a zombie suicide.) Zombies are merely open to the **possibility** of another death. They accept it as part of the general condition of being a zombie, and do not allow it to deter them from their efforts to eat the brains of as many humans as possible.

Throughout military history (which is to say, history), soldiers have erred by confusing acceptance of the possible outcome of death with killing themselves. The examples of this are some of the most ill-advised tactics in recorded warfare. The use of the much-celebrated kamikaze pilots (of both airplanes and submarines) used by Japan in World War II is regarded by contemporary military historians as one of the largest

I have not yet begun to fight. Because now I'm a living human. But later, when I get reanimated as a drooling, teeth-gnashing, brain-eating zombie? Yeah, that's when most of the ass-kicking will go down, really.

blunders of the Japanese campaign. The expenditure of the kamikaze program in resources, morale, and human cost never created military victories or gains to offset the costs. And the most dishonorable, failed combatant of all might be the contemporary suicide bomber. This person can hardly be said to be engaging in "combat" at all. Further, the negative public sentiment generated by the use of suicide bombers has the strength to turn the entire Western world against any entity employing them. A country or political group has to be pretty far gone and/or insane to employ suicide bombers.

There is, however, much to be learned from examples of warriors who have accepted situations in which death is likely, **but not certain.** Indeed, the greatest military accomplishments in history tend to be achieved when it appears that death is all but certain, but soldiers find a way to fight on.

If your goal is to fight with the effectiveness of a zombie, then commence each battle with the mantra: "I am already dead."

(If you're an actual zombie, then this will already be true.) Your "being dead" does not excuse you (as it might an actual corpse) from obeying superior officers, carrying out your orders, or other battlefield responsibilities. However, it will empower you to carry out any military task—even under the most harrowing enemy fire—with the steely-eyed resolve of a zombie. This will make you a more effective soldier, which will allow you to do things like kill the enemy before he kills you. I say with no irony that "being dead" will very much assist you in staying alive.

5

Be Independent

Okay, first of all, as a zombie soldier, you are not in charge. You still have to obey orders and answer to a commanding officer. (If you want to be a leader on the zombie battlefield, then skip to the second half of this book.)

The key to a zombie soldier's superior performance in the chain of command is this rule: **Obey orders, but don't require them.**

When a zombie is attacking a group of fearful, lost tourists on some kind of tropical island, it doesn't need to be told what to do all the time. There is no micromanagement of zombies. A zombie can stalk and kill the tourists one by one with pretty much no prompting at all. However, if another zombie suddenly (or some kind of zombie-creating voodoo priest) shows up and gives it some new ideas about how it could better dispatch the tasty humans, then sure, it's going to follow along with its peers. But the point is that it doesn't *need* to.

The "default setting" for a zombie—and for a zombie soldier—is "murderous carnal mayhem." A commander employing zombies in the battlefield needs to always be able to count on you for this. His troops must—without prompting—be inclined to attack whatever enemy is nearest at all times.

Thus, if you want to fight like a zombie, you may need to rev up your default setting. For most contemporary soldiers, this would be "standing at attention" (if superiors are looking) or "just lounging around" (if superiors *aren't* looking). However, few soldiers, when left without direct orders from the top, would take it upon themselves to constantly hunt for something to kill. This is what needs to be changed.

You need to make your default setting closer to that of an actual zombie. When you have no specific orders to advance, and your commanders have said things like "sit tight" or "hold position," you need to interpret that to mean: "Constantly seek and kill the enemy."

A zombie soldier should be a force that can be unleashed on an enemy entrenchment with no further communication needed. Ideally, one should be able to drop zombie soldiers off—like out of helicopters or something—and trust that they'll get the job done with no need for constant communication. ("Come in,

HQ. We ate their brains . . . over.") When deployed in a hostile environment with no enemies immediately visible, conventional soldiers tend to bivouac and wait for orders. Zombie soldiers tend to hit the ground looking for an enemy to kill.

One thing that makes zombie soldiers superior to conventional soldiers is their ability to attack without prompting. (Conventional soldiers tend to waste valuable attacking time waiting around for "a battle plan" and similar things.) Consider the following comparisons.

If cut off from communications with HQ:

Conventional soldiers *will hold position and attempt to reestablish lines of communication.*

Zombie soldiers *will hunt and kill the enemy.*

If caused to encounter unforeseen obstacles, natural disasters, or confusing signs from the enemy:

Conventional soldiers *will wait for word from senior command on how they ought to proceed in light of this new development.*

Zombie soldiers *will hunt and kill the enemy.*

If faced with an overwhelming foe they cannot possibly hope to defeat themselves:

Conventional soldiers *will call for reinforcements, request an air strike, or just run away.*

Zombie soldiers *will hunt and kill the enemy.*

See a pattern here?

Not to belabor the point, but soldiers who are groomed to be utterly reliant on commanders and "orders" tend to be unable to think for themselves and to act of their own accord when the time is right for that sort of thing. What for a zombie might be "taking initiative" (attacking an encampment of enemies at first sight, suddenly changing course when humans are spotted, making sure to eat people's brains) can mean a court-martial for soldiers in most armies around the world. At this point you have to ask yourself: **Do you want to "be conventional," or do you want to win battles?** The choice is yours, tough guy. You can spend all day concentrating on fitting into a rigorously enforced "chain of command" where epaulets and shoulder stripes dictate who can or cannot act with authority, or you can spend all day ruling the battlefield as a zombie soldier, striking fear into your enemies, and **kicking ass without being told to.**

This model isn't proposing some kind of "military communism" where every soldier is equal. (Besides, have you ever seen communist soldiers? They are the least autonomous, most rank-obsessed group you could come across. As often as not, they are paralyzed into inaction for fear of doing the wrong thing or upsetting a superior. [This is the opposite of zombie soldiers, who are never paralyzed—except maybe by magic, or some kind of freeze-ray—and who take as given that most of their actions are going to upset people, but just say "fuck it" and go ahead anyway.]) Rather, it instills a notion that whatever a soldier's rank or station (or state of utter desiccation and decrepitude), there are some activities that connect all of them.

Finally, think about a zombie in its natural state. Forget battlefield scenarios for a moment, and start at the Haitian graveyard, moss-covered family crypt, or lonely potter's field where the zombie takes its first steps into the world of the walking dead. That zombie already has all it needs to function effectively in the world it inhabits: teeth (probably at least a few), claws (in most cases), and an insatiable desire to consume human brains (definitely). There is no additional "instruction" needed for this zombie to function effectively. The voodoo priest, mad scientist, or *Necronomicon* enthusiast who has brought the zombie into being knows full well that he can count on the zombie to "do what zombies do" with no tutelage or micromanagement.

If you want to be a zombie soldier and an asset to whatever cause you serve, make certain that you give your commanding officers the reliable independence of a zombie. Demonstrate to them what you like to do (find and kill the enemy) and that you can do it with no prompting or instruction. Only then will you find yourself truly put to optimal use on the battlefield.

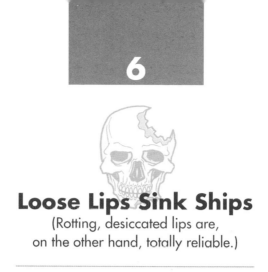

Loose Lips Sink Ships

(Rotting, desiccated lips are,
on the other hand, totally reliable.)

Let's face it; it doesn't take much to fuck up a mission. The slightest change in weather can postpone the launch of a multimillion-dollar rocket. Choppy seas can delay (or destroy) a nautical offensive. Rioting indigenous people can totally muck up your army's plans to occupy their land and take their shit. As a zombie soldier, you always want to eliminate as many of these external factors as possible to ensure smooth sailing for whatever nefarious military offensive you are planning. And the *last thing* you ever need is for invasion plans or attack stratagems to be compromised because people heard you talking about them.

One of the advantages a zombie soldier must possess is a knack for complete silence regarding matters pertaining to the battlefield. This is even true **while on the battlefield itself.**

49

Zombies are known for being quiet, but are not all completely silent. The walking dead are known moaners and groaners, and probably more than half of them can articulate at least one word ("brains"). Some higher-functioning zombies can even string together complete sentences or intentionally impersonate humans. The fact remains, however, that zombies **never talk more than is necessary.** There is no zombie chitchat. There is no banter around the campfire (or the mausoleum or whatever). Zombies have no need to "talk about the weather" (literally or figuratively) with their compatriots. This silence may be due to factors such as a lack of lips and functional vocal cords, but even zombies rendered silent by uncooperative physiology **still do not attempt to communicate with their colleagues through other means.** This, then, suggests that a zombie's lack of impulse to communicate stems from something deeper. I wish to posit here that they don't need to chat with one another, **because zombies (and zombie armies) already have a really excellent esprit de corps(e).** Most people chat idly in order to establish a rapport with people they are still getting to know and trust. But zombies have such complete camaraderie that this is never necessary. A zombie's natural silence is more than a nice thing to have on covert missions. It is one of the most important keys to the success of the zombie warrior.

Because they don't go around discussing things like attack plans and "next steps" on the battlefield, zombies never betray anything that might give an opposing army an advantage. There is no point to spying or eavesdropping on zombies. No one has ever sent a secret agent, dressed as a member of the walking dead, to infiltrate a zombie camp to see what could be learned from the zombie soldiers. (And no Mata Hari femmes fatales have ever initiated liaisons with a zombie commander to see what could be learned.)

A zombie's silence is not limited to preparations; zombies are mostly silent on the battlefield, too. However, this doesn't mean that they can't communicate when it's absolutely necessary. Zombies **do** communicate on the battlefield through a series of subtle, nonverbal cues. The most dominant of these may be called: "Just following the zombie in front of you." There is an elegant simplicity here. As a zombie's reasoning goes: *If a zombie is moving, it is because it sees an enemy (or food) and is moving closer to it. Therefore, if the zombie in front of me is moving, it must see an enemy/food ahead, and if I follow that zombie, then I, too, will move closer to an enemy/food.* No part of this process involves the need for spoken language.

Zombies can also moan in surprise or alarm when a new enemy is sighted. This typically indicates to surrounding zombies the appearance of the new enemy. (In many respects, a zombie's moan can be compared to the bark of a dog; it indicates the desire for something, and that others like it should know its presence.)

Finally, zombies have been known to moan out of frustration. For example, when humans have secreted themselves behind an iron door, zombies have been known to gather in front of it and emit low moans and groans. A zombie's moans of frustration are more than just a sacrilegious or pornographic exclamation of regret and anger. They are also a message to other zombies: "There is frustration and failure here. We must resolve the matter some other way." And the thing is, **they do.** If zombies have trapped a group of humans in a machine shed and find themselves groaning in front of the bolted door, some other zombie is always going to realize that that way is blocked and start looking for another way to get inside. It may tunnel under the side of the shed or it may find a weakness in the rear paneling and bust its way through it. The point is, when one zombie moans in frustration, another zombie takes it as a call to action and does something about the situation.

If you want to fight like a zombie, then work on cultivating a reputation as the quietest guy in your unit. You do not need to be completely mute—again, most zombies do talk *a bit*—but limit your speech to things unrelated to military engagements. Teach those around you to communicate nonverbally as many battlefield actions as possible. And if the guy in front of you looks like he sees something good, you can probably just follow him.

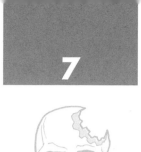

Disarming Your Enemy

You have an advantage over your enemy. As a zombie soldier, you require no weapons other than your own fingernails and incisors to be a deadly killing machine. (If other things are at hand, you can use them, sure, but you don't **require** them.)

In contrast, your enemy—faced with putting up a fight without a gun in his hand (or a bayonet at the end of it)—will likely consider himself "disarmed" when he must fight with only what God gave him. He is likely to see surrender as his only option. As a zombie, you can fight in conditions where he cannot. **This is another key to a zombie's advantage on the battlefield.**

It's not just the case that zombies win in almost every battlefield situation because they never give up and never consider themselves "disarmed." Zombies also win by convincing others that

they must surrender because they lack the adequate means to fight a zombie foe. In illustrating how zombies do this, we may have to expand your definition of "disarm."

When most people think of "disarming the enemy," they likely picture covert shock troops scaling the walls of enemy compounds and delivering karate blows to unsuspecting guards before they even have time to raise their Kalashnikovs. This manner of disarmament is certainly acceptable in some situations, but also, **it's a hell of a lot of work.** Zombies don't have the time to practice shinnying up grappling-hook ropes and perfecting silent takedown moves for days on end. Zombies have more important things to do (eating brains).

Besides, zombies prefer a direct approach to things. That's just the way they are.

Zombies have a different strategy for disarming their human foes. Namely, **they reduce their opponent's weapons option until it is equal to their own through attrition and stealth.** This works because when zombies face an equally armed foe, zombies are always going to win. As numerous anecdotal examples (and hundreds of awesome zombie movies) testify, zombies do not always win when they are outnumbered and outgunned. Yet, the more zombies there are, the more a weapons advantage is neutralized. Some examples may help solidify the point:

Scenario: One zombie versus one human.

Armament: Neither has a weapon.

Outcome: The zombie is always going to win.

Scenario: One zombie versus one human.

Armament: Human is armed with conventional weapons (shotgun, automatic rifle, grenades)

Outcome: Human is probably going to win. (Unless he/she is really a wuss or a bad shot or something.)

Scenario: Many zombies versus one human.

Armament: Again, human has conventional weapons.

Outcome: The more zombies there are, the smaller the chance the human has. He risks running out of ammunition, being surprised from behind by encroaching zombies, or simply being overwhelmed through their sheer force of numbers. (**Note:** Once the human has exhausted all ammunition, this scenario reverts to the first example in this list, and even if there is only **one** zombie still left "alive" out of a large group, it will still be one too many for the human to handle.)

Zombie soldiers (and, yes, some rare, high-functioning actual zombies) use weapons when they fight. Because of the superiority of zombie fighting tactics, however, this rule of advantage largely remains in effect. Thus:

Scenario: One zombie soldier versus one human soldier.

Armament: Both soldiers have conventional weapons.

Outcome: The zombie soldier will always win.

As long as you can create a situation where your enemy's armament is less than or equal to your own, you are going to win when you fight like a zombie.

"But how do I create that situation?" you may well ask. "What if our own weaponry is not equal to that of our foes?"

The answer is: **attrition and stealth.** Almost all modern weapons have finite reserves of ammunition. Bullets run out. Arrow quivers empty. (If you're some kind of Bronze Age warrior, contending only with spears and swords, take heart in the fact that edged weapons wear down, too.) A zombie wins not by marching to war against an enemy who is holding full ammo clips and brandishing brilliantly polished sabers. Rather, a zombie wins by assaulting its enemies when bullets have been exhausted, when swords have been hacked dull, and supplies have been exhausted generally. The trick is reducing your enemy's arsenal to this state before you begin your final, fatal assault.

Yes, this **can** be accomplished by marching endless waves of zombie soldiers at enemies. (And if you have the numbers [and prefer a simpler approach] then this may be the way to go for you.) But battle plans that call for massive troop sacrifices often don't go over well with the, you know, troops. If you're a zombie-style human soldier—and not a commander of actual zombies that are willing to follow you mindlessly—then you may benefit from a different approach to achieving disarmament.

Consider: When does an enemy's machine gun cease to fire? When it is out of bullets or overheated, true. But it also will not fire if it has **not yet been loaded.** (Nor will any firearm.) Swords cannot slice a zombie's head if they have yet to be drawn from their scabbards. Crossbow bolts must be loaded. Arrows nocked. It is this situation of unreadiness that often proves the best way to encounter a disarmed enemy.

The history of zombies in combat is the history of one group catching another unaware. When zombies attack, they do so quietly and quickly (as quickly as someone who shambles forward on rotting, kneeless legs can). Zombie armies creep up in the middle of the night when human soldiers are sleeping. They attack at 2 AM (because the enemy general has totally assumed that they will attack at dawn, like a "regular army"). Zombies suddenly appear when they are not expected, often seeming to materialize out of thin air. Zombies attack at times and places that defy convention—and then "unconventionally" eat their enemy's brains.

Thus, if marching headlong until the enemy's bullets are exhausted isn't your style, you will be relieved to find that it is no less zombie of you to instead disarm your enemies by attacking when they are unprepared.

You can generally count on an enemy to be unprepared:

- In the middle of the night
- In inclement weather
- When he is retreating
- When he has just signed a truce with you
- On religious or state holidays
- If he "doesn't believe in zombies"
- If he has just made some kind of public boast about how his new fortress is, like, totally impervious to zombies

Look for these and similar situations to exploit to your advantage. As any zombie knows, the best time to attack an enemy is when he considers himself invulnerable to attack (or at least invulnerable to attack **at this point in time**). Zombies are excellent time managers. Never pausing to rest or sleep, they show up early for battles, sieges, and all other military engagements. They show up before enemies are prepared to defend themselves, much less kill zombies. They show up before it's polite or acceptable. They conform to no conventions or codes of the battlefield.

When you calculate the optimal time to attack your enemy, think only of what conditions will allow you the greatest surprise. That way, your soldiers will surge into the enemy camp like a group of zombies that just came out of nowhere. The enemy—believing that they "can't" be attacked in this situation—will still be loading their guns, drawing their swords, or just rubbing the crust out of their eyes as your well-rested, fully equipped zombie troops begin ripping into them. Your opponent can have the fanciest, most expensive zombie-killing equipment in the world, but it will afford him no advantage at all if he is not ready to use it.

As a final thought on a zombies' knack for disarmament, I advise you to trust that when you fight like a zombie, you are being watched over by providence (or voodoo gods, devils, necromancers, or whatever entities watch over the living dead). For what else can explain the remarkable frequency with which guns jam, cannons fail to fire, and ax heads fall clean off when zombies are around? Even a cursory survey of the most famous instances of zombie attack reveals that **weapons tend not to work well around zombies for some reason.** As considered above, it may be the zombies' stealth, and it may be the zombies' ability to absorb ammunition, and it may be the zombies' tendency to attack at exactly the right time. However, one sometimes has difficulty shaking the feeling that **something else** is watching over the legions of the living dead. If this dark angel conspires to hover over your own head as you fight like a zombie soldier—plugging your enemy's guns and wetting his powder with rain—then I totally advise you to go with it, dude. 'Cause some mysterious forces are just bigger than all of you—you know?

8

Patience

When most people picture effective soldiering, they tend to envision action sequences. Soldiers doing exciting things. Running quickly from place to place. Leaping over barricades and/or into trenches. Firing machine guns at helicopters while emoting by using dramatic nonwords like "Arrrgh!" and "Yaaaaahhhhhh!"

And certainly, there *are* often situations on a battlefield in which bold action is clearly called for (for traditional soldiers and for zombie soldiers alike). Objectives must be taken. Obstacles must be crossed. But as any true military veteran will tell you, there are also situations where a soldier has to **sit fucking tight and do nothing at all.** In fact, an inability to perform *this* aspect of soldiering can render obsolete any

combat abilities one might be longing to display once the fray has begun.

You must become expert at waiting patiently if you wish to fight with the effectiveness of the walking dead.

Zombies excel at being able to wait until their murderous carnage is called for. They are infinitely patient, content to bide their time whenever inaction proves a necessary next step toward getting what they want (brains). And though they wait and even "relax" (their remaining tendons and sinews) for years at a time, they never allow a wait to compromise their ability to fight. Zombies can wait for hundreds or even thousands of years in underground crypts or forgotten labyrinths, only to "snap to attention" when a group of edible humans presents itself. They can molder in graves and crypts, sometimes taking decades to scratch their way through the walls of expensive heavy coffins and slowly excavate six feet of dirt. They can remain motionless in tar or amber for millennia without complaint, only to spring into violence and carnage the moment something frees them.

We've already covered how an asset of a zombie soldier is its ability to act without prompting and to know what to do in a variety of situations without relying on "orders from headquarters." Well, a zombie's infinite patience **contributes directly to this ability to be autonomous.** Let's make this point clear with a little comparison between conventional soldiers and zombies.

When conventional soldiers, say, fall through the fissures of a giant ice shelf and find themselves trapped on a precarious ledge two hundred feet below the arctic surface, you can pretty much count them out. They're going to radio back to HQ, saying that they need to be rescued. They're going to shoot flares up toward the icy surface. They might make camp and take inventory of their existing food supply (in preparation for what could be a long wait for rescue, **but a rescue nonetheless**). Now let's change these soldiers to zombies who've fallen through a hole in the ice while in pursuit of a delicious cadre of climate change scientists. The zombies will not radio for rescue or "sit tight" until someone comes to their aid. (Important: **Nobody, living or undead, has ever come to the "rescue" of a zombie.**) Rather, the zombies will set about climbing out of the ice fissure under their own power. If that task should prove impossible, the zombies will still keep trying until their fingers wear down to nubs and their muscles fall away or deteriorate entirely. See, when zombies have a problem, they realize that the most expeditious and, indeed, only course is for them to try to **solve it themselves.** A zombie trapped below the arctic will be patient; it will scuttle inch by inch up an ice cliff for as many months or years as it takes to get back to the surface. (And then those scientists are totally getting eaten, North Face parkas and all.)

Having patience also allows zombies to survive in situations that might not be as life-threateningly perilous as the edge of an underground ice shelf, but could nonetheless drive a conventional soldier to complete and utter insanity. Zombies can be chained to the wall of a dungeon for eternity, their only stimulus the occasional foolhardy band of adventurers seeking gold and experience points. Do these mechanically restrained zombies go mad from boredom? Do they start trying to eat people who aren't there, or develop multiple zombie personalities? Heck no. They remain in a state of constant catlike readiness, prepared to rip out the throat of the next adventurer (even if they only tend to show up at intervals of several years). Zombies stay focused on their objectives and resigned to the task at hand. They don't become anxious. They don't worry about the setbacks they face. They remain committed and they remain effective.

The effectiveness of a zombie's strategy of patient waiting is no small thing. **A zombie waits patiently in a way that does not impair or lessen its fighting acumen.** Again, consider a comparison.

Imagine that several human soldiers are stranded in the middle of a tropical rainforest. (Let's say as the consequence of a helicopter crash.) They are surrounded by hostile enemies (and equally hostile fauna) confused as to their position, and are running low on supplies. What can we expect these traditional soldiers to do in this predicament? They'll likely turn on their GPS transmitter and wait to be rescued (and hope that they aren't discovered by any hostiles in the meantime). What else will they do? **Become ineffective soldiers.** They'll conserve food and water, allowing themselves to become logy and dehydrated. They'll seek cover from possible sunstroke in the ruins of their burned-out helicopter (instead of seeking the living brains of the enemy to have for lunch). They'll start praying for deliverance instead of preying on their enemies. In this case, traditional "soldiering" dictates that troops in this situation **cease to be soldiers at all** and instead start doing things that will demonstrably lessen their own killing power. **Not so with zombies.**

Say some zombies had hitched a ride in a helicopter that crash-landed (let's be honest—in all probability, the crash was probably caused by the zombies). Once they emerge from the smoldering wreck, they aren't going to waste any time dicking around with thoughts of a rescue. They're going to patiently begin the long trek toward wherever they were headed in the helicopter (toward humans). There will be no conversion of the crash site into a temporary camp, any repurposing of flak helmets as rainwater catchment devices, and certainly no lying around and hoping that an air rescue unit appears on the horizon sometime soon.

So don't give me that "We've been waiting in this tiny deer stand/uncomfortable old bunker/river of human flotsam and offal for almost an hour now! When are we going to see some action, boss?"

Zombies have been content to lurk in low places for eternities when that was required in order to realize the optimal outcome of a combat situation (brains). Instill this lesson in yourself and the soldiers serving with you. Once they start holding themselves to the standards of zombies—and not human soldiers—they will cease to be troubled by assignments requiring extended periods of not doing anything. You will quickly earn a reputation as a terrible foe who thinks nothing of lying in wait for your enemies with a patience that seems inhuman and psychotic. (However, "inhuman and psychotic" for a human is often "So?" for a zombie.)

Make it your goal to be as infinitely patient as a zombie, and your reward itself will be infinite (or you'll at least kill a lot of guys).

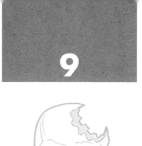

No Retreat, No Surrender

Zombies don't surrender. Everybody who fights a zombie understands that a zombie is going to fight until the very last ounce of strength is sapped from its undead body. You can set it on fire, you can blow off entire limbs, you can threaten it with all manner of torture—and still a zombie will come after you.

But here's the thing.

It's not like **some** zombies—particularly brave ones or something—don't surrender. Nope. **All** zombies don't surrender. And **this uniformity of dedication is another thing that helps ensure zombies win on the battlefield.**

Same thing goes for retreating. Even when victory looks like an impossibility . . . Even when a situation appears dire or hopeless . . . Even when retreating **would actually result in a strategic advantage of some sort** . . . zombies **never** retreat. As long as there are tasty brains waiting to be eaten on the other side of the trenches, the zombies are gonna keep bounding toward them.

If it were the case that only **most** of the zombies in a battalion would sally forth against impossible odds, then opposing generals might spend some time attempting to take prisoners, negotiating truces, or using propaganda to scare the zombies away. Opposing generals don't do this because they know it would be an utter waste of effort.

Zombies will not retreat, no matter what. This fact has a positive effect (for the zombies) of further demoralizing anybody they are fighting. For example, in many cases, soldiers will hope to "fight to a truce" or "fight until both sides are exhausted" or "fight until it's clear to the other guys that they can't possibly win." However, because zombies are inexhaustible fighting machines that don't make (or even fully understand) truces, it is not possible to treat with them, exhaust them, or get them to see the inevitable futility of making war. When you face zombies, one thing is sure: they will keep coming until either you are dead or they are destroyed.

In addition to terrifying their enemies, a zombie's inability to cease fighting when things look grim has led to some of the most startling upset victories in the history of war. In professional sports, when a media "expert" makes the wrong call about who will win a particular contest, you'll hear them backpedal by using the expression: "Well, that's why we play the games."

Why we play the games indeed.

Appearances can be deceiving and battle tides can break. Armies that appear to be weak can turn out to be strong and vice versa. The point is, just like a zombie, you've got to play the game. (Note: While zombies don't actually "play games"— maybe they could accidentally, like, kick a soccer ball or something, but that's it—they do always make a point to see things through to the end.) And rather than playing badminton or golf, zombies choose instead to be a part of the "eternal contest." Zombies compete in the epic battle of the forces of life versus the forces of death. Plus, when zombies win, they get to eat brains. (Kind of makes your gold-colored plastic trophy look like a little piece of crap, huh?)

Zombies are awesome and win more battles than anyone because they never disengage and always see things through to the end. Why do zombies adopt such a brave, all-or-nothing approach? Because it wouldn't make sense for them to surrender, call truces, or disengage at any point in a battle. The reasons armies do these things just don't apply to zombies. Consider it. Armies typically disengage/surrender/retreat:

- To live to fight another day (Zombies are already dead.)
- To "regroup" (Zombies always attack as a group.)
- To reevaluate their approach and/or come up with another plan of attack (Zombies always have the same attack plan, no matter what; they march directly toward their enemies and kill them.)
- To rest (Zombies require no rest.)
- To bury the dead (Whatever, dude. When you're already a stinking, rotting walking corpse, you get a lot less sentimental about what happens to the corpses around you.)

If you want to fight like a zombie, take these items off your menu. Never retreat or stop attacking—even if things appear to be going badly. The only condition for a battle being "over" should be that all of your enemies are dead.

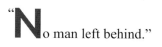

10

Selfishness Is the New Selflessness

"**N**o man left behind."

It's a motto that has long served some of the most impressive and storied fighting forces on the planet. It also doesn't apply to zombies at all.

Zombies, as everyone knows, are constantly left behind on the battlefield. One reason for this is that they tend to move slowly and often just get outpaced. But another reason is that zombies don't stop to bury their dead. Nor do they pause to tend to their wounded. Since time immemorial, soldiers facing zombies have known that it is bootless to wound one zombie in hope that others will stop to "help" it.

Thus, to become a true zombie warrior, you must expunge from your brain all fealty to the credo "No man left behind." Don't believe for one moment that zombies don't stop to attend to the fallen because they are insensitive or heartless (though, yes, some zombies are technically missing hearts). Rather, a zombie soldier understands that **the best way to help a fallen colleague is to eat the brain of the one who felled it.**

Why is it the "best way"? Consider the following:

There is no way a zombie can "help" a fellow zombie that has just had its head blown into a thousand pieces by some kind of ion cannon. Zombies are either "alive" (in a manner of speaking) or "dead" (in a manner of speaking). They're on the rampage and hunting for brains, or they've received a head shot (or other fatal injury) and have returned to being motionless corpses. **There is no such thing as a wounded zombie.** Hence, in a zombie army, you will find no medics stopping to tend to the fallen.

The fact of there being no real concept of "rank" in a zombie army makes it unnecessary—and, indeed, impossible—for a zombie to strive to protect a commander. (This desire to protect commanders may be the most common scenario in which human soldiers choose to act "selflessly.") Certainly, any cursory student of military history can name a dozen instances of brave soldiers taking great pains—or even sacrificing themselves—to protect fallen generals from flying shrapnel or cannonballs. This makes no sense for zombies (or zombie soldiers) because all zombies have the same rank: Zombie.

Zombies are good at surprise attacks and at showing up when they're not expected. However, when zombies **are** targeted in the crosshairs, there is almost no missing them. Zombies have accepted the fact that you're out to kill them. There are no zombie "evasive maneuvers." They will slouch forward slowly and allow an enemy to carefully draw a bead for as long as he likes. They will linger in open fields, eschewing cover or tactical advantages the terrain might afford. When enemy fire begins to make the dirt at their feet dance with bullets, they will not run for cover. **They will only continue to advance toward the enemy.** A zombie has accepted the fact that your next bullet might have its name on it. Or its neighbor's name. There is no room for "selflessness" here. But whether it dies or its neighbor dies, one of then is **still** coming for you.

Zombies are invulnerable to psychological attack. There are no undead versions of Tokyo Rose, Lord Haw-Haw, or Axis Sally. Capturing and torturing defenseless zombies (like those without fingernails and teeth) in order to enrage or humiliate a zombie army will be a completely ineffective project. A zombie's lack of concern for its compatriots affords it the strategic advantage of never becoming rattled or jarred into hasty action when an enemy baits it. Zombies don't care about other zombies—at least not when compared with how much they care about **eating you.**

When honing your own zombie fighting skills, be sure to cultivate within yourself a complete lack of concern for wounded or fallen soldiers on your own side. Again, this is not because you "don't care about them." It is because you have realized that the best way to honor their memory or soothe the pain of their injuries is to **keep attacking and take out whomever attacked them.** Your constant, ceaseless, zombielike plod forward will be a testament to the fealty and brotherhood you share with the men and women writhing in pools of blood next to you.

Remember: Instead of "No man left behind," a zombie's creed is "No. Man left behind."

I hope you can keep that straight.

11

Intel Is Everything . . .
So Withhold It from
Your Enemy

(In other words, be mysterious.)

Today's soldiers wage war with the most powerful weapon of all: nuclear bombs. But failing those, most agree that **information** is probably the best thing you can use to help your side win the fight. On the flip side of that coin, withholding information from your enemy is an excellent way to help him lose the fight.

Soldiers throughout history have understood this truth and made considerable bets accordingly. In the Revolutionary War, Nathan Hale risked (and eloquently forfeited) his life by sneaking into British-held territory and putting sketches of their troop locations in his shoes. And what is the history of aviation if not the history of the search for military information? The superpowers of today employ expensive satellite imaging to learn the exact locations of enemy troops and send unmanned drones crisscrossing through desert landscapes to beam back live infrared video feeds showing enemy troops and locations.

Though zombies tend not to employ technology to **find** their enemies, they are natural experts at baffling any and all measures used by enemies **to find them.** Zombies' lack of internal body temperature makes infrared imaging useless on them. The earth tones of a zombie's rotting body (black, blue-black, sickly brown, etc.) serve as a natural camouflage. A zombie's slow gait ensures that it fails to register on most motion-sensing computers.

And people still wonder: "Where the fuck did all these zombies suddenly come from!?"

The zombies didn't magically appear. **You just didn't see them coming.**

If you want to take away your enemy's preparedness, then remove his information—especially information about **you.** Even after their presence is detected on the battlefield, zombies are masters of stymieing their enemies because so little is known about them. An enemy confronted with a zombie foe may suddenly wonder:

How did they come to be?

Was it a secret government experiment gone wrong? The consequences of a university professor's research into the *Necronomicon*? Perhaps some sort of virus from outer space?

Nobody's going to be able to tell you, because they won't know. A foe with mysterious origins is a foe you don't want to mess with.

How can we kill them?

Will a bullet to the brain do the trick, or must I separate the head from the body entirely? If blasted apart by a claymore mine, will the resulting parts continue attacking on their own? If set ablaze with flamethrowers, will the zombies disintegrate or simply become even more dangerous "flaming zombies," setting our camp on fire as they advance?

What do they want?

To eat my brain? (Er . . . oh yeah. I guess that one **is** simple.)

And in between these big questions is a lot of ambiguity that zombies bring to the table. Will electricity destroy them? What about a Taser? Is it possible to distract or confuse them, or will they always remain focused? An experienced quartermaster can be completely flummoxed by zombies and spend hours trying to guess if any of the impressive-looking weapons in his storehouse are going to be any good at all against the oncoming horde.

The point is: With zombies, you just don't know.

Thus, to enjoy the benefits of a zombie on the battlefield, you need to cultivate an air of mystery about yourself. Consider the following areas that can be infused with the quixotic and unexplainable to best effect:

Your motivations

Your tactics

Your strengths and weaknesses

First off, why are you attacking? (Unless you're just violent and mercurial, which is fine, you probably already have an answer.) Is there some sort of historical vendetta you're trying to settle? Was there recently an incursion by militants that another nation hasn't done a good job of containing 'cause really, they secretly approve of everything the militants do? Whatever they are, keep your motivations secret from your enemies for as long as possible. This will make your army seem less a reasoning, thinking thing with goals than a force of nature—mindless but awesomely powerful and unable to be reasoned with.

Your tactics, too, should be a subject of mystery. As previously noted, a zombie soldier's main "tactic" is to charge the enemy headlong and kill until all of them are dead. But the first time he engages you, your opponent has no way of knowing that this is how you intend to fight. They may assume that your troops are all massed in one slavering mob in the center of the battle-field as some kind of ploy. Could the rows and rows of lightly armed infantry that you present be concealing some sort of secret weapon? Does the lumbering, awkward gait at which you "charge" denote some special formation to come? Again, your opponent will have no way of knowing. Fight like a zombie, sure, but allow your fighting style to confuse your enemy.

Cloaking your strengths and weaknesses in a patina of mystery and deception is also a valuable step on the road to victory. Just as an opposing general looks into a giant horde of mangy zombies and wonders, "Are my catapults going to be of any use at all against these things?" so must **you** inspire confusion and cause your opponents to doubt themselves. A good place to start is with clothing. Can you wear a bio-suit or at least some kind of weird-looking helmet? This will look pretty cool (inspiring, like, morale and stuff) and befuddle your opponents. Do those suits protect against chemical attack? Do those helmets have built-in night vision goggles or are they purely a protective measure? Your enemy won't know. But you will, and that's the point. Even if you take the battlefield covered in spray-painted Hefty bags and tinfoil hats, an important objective will have been achieved before the first shot is ever fired. The enemy will be wondering: "What the hell is going on here?"

A confused enemy is a tentative, ineffective one, who will allow you to kill him all the more easily. Anything you can do to make your actions or mien more incomprehensible in battle will add to the effectiveness of your fighting. Experiment with it, be creative, and let a zombie be your model. Stumble. Moan. Drool. **And then kick everyone's ass.**

12

Fight with "Honor"

"It is not enough to win.
One must win honorably."

Since the earliest days of war, this solemn precept has driven soldiers to comport themselves in such a way that they can be counted as having fought "honorably." Most warriors seek to fight with honor because they believe it will help their victories—and consequent domination of the populace—to be perceived as legitimate. (The thinking goes that it's one thing for conquered peoples to accept it when their best warriors fight your best warriors and their guys get their asses kicked fair and square, but it's another when you defeat their solders through dishonorable trickery or subterfuge.)

However, zombies don't care how they're remembered. (Zombies have trouble remembering what they did last week, much less who won a battle years ago and if they fought honorably.) Zombies also don't attack a city for the purpose of occupying it or installing themselves as rulers. (It's more for the purpose of lunch, really.)

Yet in military academies across all nations, soldiers are taught that honor is the most prized asset of any soldier. They are told that it alone is what connects them to the founding patriots of their democracy/dictatorship/hastily installed military regime.

But is it *really*?

Here's a shocking truth: The most patriotic and successful soldiers of yesteryear **were** like you . . . but not because they were obsessed with honor. Rather, they were like you because they **did what they had to do to win battles.** Period. Later—after the fact—their style of fighting (whatever it was they used) was deemed "honorable" because these patriots had used it. This retroactive assignment of "honor" to different military situations is key to the perpetuation of patriotic myth. If you actually want to emulate your country's heroes, you need to just focus on doing whatever it takes to win battles. Don't worry about honor. Honor will come later.

As a zombie soldier, **you must fight within your own definition of "honor."** This is because the zombie is largely excluded from honor-granting institutions the world over. There are few military arbiters anywhere who will say anything other than: "All zombies are dishonorable." (If they are allowed to expound and expand, they'll probably add something like: "Also, they're dirty, rotting corpses that should be destroyed on sight!") Thus, you may have to become your own authority on what is and isn't honorable.

Here's a hint: **if it helps your side win the battle, then it's honorable.** Like I said before, almost anything can be called "honorable" after the fact. For example:

Sneaking up behind an unarmed enemy soldier during an armistice and viciously eating his brain? A selfless patriotic act.

Disguising yourself as a piece of floating offal and capsizing a raft full of people, upon whom you then feast? An act of honor and dignity.

Bursting into flame (probably because people were throwing firebombs at you) and stumbling into an enemy armory you then set alight? A self-sacrifice worthy of Nathan Hale in its eloquence.

See? Easy, innit?

If you want to fight like a zombie and fight to win, "honor" should be the last thing on your mind on the day of the battle. However, your enemy **should be encouraged to consider honor at every possible turn.** If you can help your foe become preoccupied with engaging your side in an honorable way, it will limit his options and stymie his willingness to unleash all of his weapons at full capacity.

One easy way to do this is to affect a guise known as **"the Pitiful Zombie."** I mean, you're a zombie. There's no hiding that. You and your fellows are a bunch of moldering cadavers with mouths dripping fresh blood. Your enemy will be able to see this a mile away (literally, through his binoculars). But many more terrible and terrifying figures than zombies have been made to seem pitiful or pitiable. Consider the psychotic killer—butcherer of entire families—paraded before the court as a sufferer of "mental illness" who can't help that he constantly hears voices telling him to kill. Consider the Bengal tigers that have marauded through the Indian countryside killing entire villages: the square-jawed naturalist is quick to remind the viewer of the nature documentary that these animals are simply "doing what comes naturally" and "acting according to their instincts." If psychos and tigers can catch a break, then why can't zombies? (**Answer:** They can.) If you know your enemy to be preoccupied with honor, make sure that he receives intelligence such that you and your compatriots are "stupid, insensible creatures" who were "reanimated against your will" to walk the earth and search for brains. Couch yourselves as victims of a terrible hunger that drives you to commit horrible acts (which you would otherwise **never** think of doing), as slaves to a horrible need. Addicts. This will cause the enemy general—even as he engages you—to take pity on you and consider your slaughter as dishonorable as the killing of a mentally disabled person or a wild animal that "cannot help it."

Meanwhile, you will help yourselves to your enemy's brains.

Some of the greatest missteps of modern warfare have arisen from this impulse to "preserve honor" by failing to attack enemy soldiers who were presented as pitiable. At the end of the first Iraq War, Colin Powell and Norman Schwarzkopf failed to invade the city of Baghdad and capture Saddam Hussein. This was not because they couldn't have easily done this. Rather, they felt that their victories to date had been so overwhelming—and the enemy soldiers punished so brutally— that to continue on to the capital would involve a dishonorable amount of further carnage. Who can blame them for thinking this way? (**Answer:** Zombies, who are never, ever concerned with honor or "being mean" to the enemy.) A traditional military preoccupation with "fighting the good fight" meant that we "had to go back and fucking do it all over again" in 2003.

Use this widespread sensibility against your enemy by positioning the killing of zombies as a regrettable and dishonorable thing. Then spring into combat and fight with little to no compunction of your own. The combined effect will be just another set of factors that always help zombie armies win.

PART II

How to Lead Like a Zombie

Physical prowess, mental toughness, and steady nerves are tools required of the modern-day soldier. But for those who would **lead** others into combat, something more is required. In a word: **brains.**

Those who aspire to the general's rank must understand the great responsibility that comes along with the charge. Commanders must seek to win military engagements quickly, decisively, and with as little unnecessary loss of life as possible—on their side, at least. Those who would seek to command zombies take on the ultimate mantle of responsibility that comes with using the living dead in combat against humans (or bears or aliens . . . really, whatever you like).

The Zombie Commander must be unflappable. When the news is bad, he must embrace the information with a zombie's thoughtful stoicism. When the intel is good, and the enemies are driven from the field before him, his response must likewise be measured and reserved. Zombies are not creatures given to extreme emotion. To howl in victory or sob in defeat is to break the zombie code.

> **Veni. Vidi. Zombi!**
>
> **(I came. I saw. What I saw was zombies, so I broke the fuck out!)** Expect your army to inspire terror in even the most intrepid and esteemed emperors. Those who have previously succeeding simply by "coming, seeing, and conquering" are going to think fucking twice before they tango with an army of zombies.

A Zombie Commander must, like his troops, be brave and stalwart. He must be able to send his troops into battle with armies ten times the size of his own. He must not blanch (except as a function of blood loss) at the task before him, even when required to take towering citadels, remote mountaintop fortifications, or entire armadas at sea. He must lead with confidence and inspire confidence in those who serve him.

Now, a shocking statement: **Strictly speaking, while there may be Zombie Commanders, there are no "zombie commanders."**

You heard me. No zombie commanders. No zombie leaders. No zombie marshals capable of actually, technically marshalling zombies. (Now and then, a high-ranking military officer will be reanimated as a zombie in full dress uniform—which is, of course, hilarious—but it's not like it's barking orders to the other zombies around him.)

There are no zombie commanders because zombies will not be commanded. They are obstreperous, independent things. Yell at a zombie all you want—or have a drill sergeant bark at a zombie till he's blue in the face—it's not going to change one darn thing the zombie does. The walking dead are immune to the verbal barbs and identifications of their shortcomings that might motivate a human soldier to charge once more into the breach (or at least to stay in formation). Point out to a zombie that its posture sucks, that it's got a big belly, and that a worm is—at this very moment—crawling out of its nose. The zombie won't even flinch. (It will, however, try to eat you.)

And yet—here emerges the irony—a stinking horde of uncommandable zombies are far superior to almost any fighting force on earth. Their ability to sustain incredible amounts of damage, to dish our fierce attacks, and to generally terrorize the populace of whatever city they are attacking is virtually unrivaled in recorded military history. Individually, the members of this fighting force are self-centered, smelly, and averse to suggestion (much less command). But as a group, they are an efficient fighting force that generals the world 'round can only envy. Yet it is not discipline, or even what can be called intentionality, that moves their awesome murderousness from objective to objective. Instead, it is an irresistible drive to feast on the still-thinking brains of the living.

To attempt to command an army of human soldiers in such a way that they shall fight with the uncanny excellence of zombies, one must do a kind of zombie-phenomenology. One cannot ask what zombie commanders are thinking. (Again, there are no zombie commanders. [And if there were, and they were thinking, it would just be about how to get some brains.]) Rather, one must observe the way armies of zombies tend to conquer and kill so effectively, and from these instances extract as many individual lessons as possible.

A would-be Zombie Commander must ask:

How do zombies connect to decimate enemies so utterly?

How is it that, time and again, a smaller force of zombies can invariably defeat a much larger foe?

There are frequently more zombies than brains to go around, so how is infighting avoided?

It is only by studying the aspects of a zombie fighting force that the secrets to its efficacy can be learned and adopted. Yet, if it is undertaken with the clear mind and unblinking eye of a zombie, you will find that such a study can be illuminating and fruitful. The secrets of the zombie army are ranged here before you.

Let's begin by considering how they move.

13

The Lost Art of Always Just Marching Straight Ahead

Sometimes people assume that battlefield techniques lacking in complexity must be outdated and ineffective. People are attuned to watch for the new, the surprising, the cutting edge (or leading edge, or bleeding edge, or the edge of a zombie's teeth as it eats you). People are ready to credit a complicated tactic with being able to accomplish wonderful things but are suspicious of an approach known for its "elegant simplicity."

Sometimes the best ways of doing things **are** the oldest and simplest. **There are some models upon which no improvements can be made.** And one such a model is the attack pattern of the zombie (**a.k.a.:** the first thing you must learn if you are to become a Zombie Commander).

A zombie army is always moving. (Not at the quick step, certainly, but they're always making forward progress.) Moving brings you closer to the enemy. Moving makes things happen. Moving keeps things interesting.

Zombie soldiers neither bivouac nor "hold their position." If a zombie army isn't moving, it's because humans are nearby and the zombies are trying to figure out how to get at them. Yet the main function of this tactic is not merely to locate the enemy and have a nice change of scenery. Always Just Marching Straight Ahead will endow your soldiers with numerous **advantages on the battlefield** once combat begins.

The first opportunity for this strategy to help you will be the moment your army first comes into contact with the enemy forces. Throughout history, large armies have tended to "make camp" once sighting their enemies—pausing to consider a plan of attack, determining how the terrain might best be used, and sizing up the enemy's strengths and weaknesses. (Sometimes, based on an unfavorable analysis of the latter, the armies elect not to engage one another at all!) Weapons are prepared. Battle plans are drawn. On some occasions, representatives from the two sides actually meet face-to-face to see if the conflict can be avoided (and, if it's unavoidable, then they discuss the "rules" and parameters of the upcoming engagement).

When you locate an enemy army to engage, you will do **none of these things. You** are not a typical commander, and **you are**

not commanding a typical army. That is why you will win the day and crush your enemy utterly.

When a horde of zombies comes on some tasty humans, the horde doesn't draw up a plan of attack. It doesn't wait till dawn because doing so is poetic or traditional. It just attacks. Then and there. It could be dawn's first light or two in the morning. It could be sunny, stormy, foggy, raining locusts, or earth-quaking. Zombies don't care. They will still attack.

There is **never** any reason for a zombie to delay combat. When you go into battle like a zombie, you and your troops will be ready to fight on a moment's notice and require no preparations to be able to stagger into combat in optimal fighting shape. Your enemy will not be thus prepared. Your enemy expects (and probably even **requires**) a brief period in which to transition troops from "marching army" to "fighting army." Little does he know, zombies are both of those things at the same time. At all times. Always.

By Always Just Marching Straight Ahead, you will find yourself attacking enemies who are unprepared, confused, and shocked. This policy will also provide the tactical advantage of eliminating any of the defensive measures your enemy might be accustomed to deploying before a battle. He may be expecting to dig trenches, set up barbed wire, plant land mines, or construct elaborate siege devices. A good percentage of the army marching with him may not even be soldiers at all, but rather battlefield engineers skilled at putting these devices in place. But no matter how skilled these engineers are, they aren't going to have any time to go to work (which will essentially reduce them to "useless flotsam waiting to be eaten by zombies").

Always Just Marching Straight Ahead also gives you an advantage when it comes to troop movement. Your opponent will be baffled by the simplicity of your tactics and will not understand how to react. (When he finally realizes, "Oh, gee, they always just marched straight ahead, didn't they?" it will be too late, and his brain will be eaten.)

For example, your enemy will probably be counting on you to approach him by using cover and positions affording protection from fire. He will thus concentrate his attentions on these positions (which you will never even occupy).

He will be counting on you to try to take the "high ground" that gives you the best position from which to attack him. He will have reinforced these high-value positions accordingly. You will ignore them completely.

Your enemy will be attuned to any sign of misdirection, feints, and counterattacks. He will, therefore, be surprised when your whole army uses none of them, and instead just comes right at his center, all at once.

He will—until he starts to think about their win-loss record— also probably be prejudiced against zombies, and fail to credit a group of soldiers attacking him in a zombie fashion as any real threat. He will be sorely mistaken.

In short, your enemy has every reason in the world to believe that Always Just Marching Straight Ahead is what you are **not** going to do. But you're going to do it, and you're going to kick his ass in the process. You're going to overwhelm his line and attack his nerve center. He'll see too late that you **don't care** about taking positions of tactical significance, gaining the higher ground, or concentrating on high-value targets. You're just a marauding group of zombies, and you're coming straight at him. In these days of "modern warfare" when generals win by anticipating what their enemies will want out of an engagement, you will win by having different objectives than anyone he's seen before on any field of combat. (It's impossible to "guess several moves ahead" in the chess game of battle if your opponent isn't even after the king.) You want to get your soldiers in biting distance of his solders as expeditiously as possible. You want to overwhelm him as quickly as possible, whether or not this subjects your troops to fire. You understand that the shortest distance between your teeth and his brain is a straight line. If he has any questions about that, he can ask them personally when you storm his headquarters and eat his head like a melon.

Note: When preparing your troops to adopt this fighting style, it is important to remind them that the third word in the tactic is "Marching" not "Sprinting like a goddamned hermaphrodite Olympian." While some zombies *are* faster than others,

zombies achieve optimal effectiveness in a group by consti-
tuting a small part of a giant mass of writhing, biting flesh
that moves inexorably toward the enemy at all times. (Plus, if
your troops are humans acting like zombies—and not actual
zombies—then they are liable to get tired if you just run them
everywhere constantly.) This slow, steady movement will
further add to your battlefield prowess by inspiring terror in
your enemy. When your soldiers head directly for the opposing
troops with the confident, unhurried gait of zombies, the enemy
soldiers are liable to think: "We're being attacked **slowly**?
What the fuck is up with **that**?" Then they are going to soil
themselves because they'll realize that they are facing zombies
or troops who fight like zombies (which are very much the
same thing when you're going into battle against them).

In conclusion, Always Just Marching Straight Ahead is an
awesome battlefield tactic, because it baffles your enemies,
forces them to fight before they're ready, and makes the battle
happen faster. Also, it's pretty easy for your troops to remember.
If they get confused in the thick of battle or something, they'll
be like: "What was that **one** maneuver I needed to execute on
the battlefield today . . . oh yeah. Always Just March Straight
Ahead." And if your soldiers can't remember that, then maybe
we need to work on your recruiting.

14

Occupation

Let's say your army wins a decisive battle (by Always Just Marching Straight Ahead) and has gained control of a major city formerly belonging to your enemy. You may have won the day against the enemy's troops, but that doesn't mean you've "won" the city itself. Why not? Because you still have to deal with occupying it.

Under most circumstances, once it takes control of a city and drives the defending army out of it, an invading army has to stay inside that city or risk losing it. You can't just raise your flag in the town square, vacate the next day, and expect the place to somehow remain under your military control. The residents who remain (though they may have welcomed you as "liberators" and even thrown a ticker-tape parade) likely still harbor some resentment toward you for being there, and a certain percentage of them will *always* remain loyal to the old regime. If your army departs from a city with an inadequate troop presence left behind, it will take no great effort for these loyalists to reach out to your opponents, and—*boom!*—they combine forces to retake the city from you.

For centuries, military leaders have struggled with how to resolve this problem. You can take one of your enemy's cities and occupy it, sure. But what if he has other cities that you *also* want? Move your army out of the first city to attack the second, and his forces will take the first one back over again.

Contemporary military strategists deal with this ancient quandary by speaking of the need to "win the hearts and minds" of indigenous residents in whatever locale you've conquered. They advocate exercises that build trust between local leaders and members of your occupying force. They encourage investing in the infrastructure of conquered cities, using occupying soldiers to build new roads and construct new bridges—the idea being that that the local residents will feel you've made a real investment in their community, and that you view it as more than just a place you've conquered.

But see, zombies don't win hearts and minds. They eat them.

And one of the advantages to waging war like a zombie is that you **never** have to deal with these unpleasant options usually foisted onto an occupying force.

Sure, you'll occupy enemy towns, cities, and entire countries when you fight like a zombie. And yeah, you'll use force to make it happen. However, when you truly fight like a zombie, the regulation of the civilian population in captured areas largely becomes a nonissue. Though it may sound hard to believe, when you fight like a zombie, **these populations will regulate themselves for you.**

For example, when an army of zombies—let's say several thousand strong—is sighted approaching a population center, the residents of that population center (civilian and military alike) have two choices. They can flee or they can stay and fight. (Nothing remarkable so far, right? This is the case when *any* enemy begins to engage a city.) If they choose to stay and fight, then the city will fall under siege from the zombies. But fighting zombies is an all-or-nothing proposition, so if the defense of the city appears to be going *badly*, then **all of the residents are going to make some kind of break for it.** Nobody is going to stay behind and try to flatter the occupying zombies, or angle to be appointed the new Vichy ruler of the grim necropolis that will shortly rise up all around them.

When zombies occupy a city, it ceases to bear any resemblance to its former self (or, indeed, to any city run by humans). All the humans leave or are eaten. The town sign may be amended to read "Population: Just Zombies." While most conquering armies allow a captured populace to maintain some sort of self-governance (by appointing leaders friendly to the occupation), zombie armies do away with representative government entirely by eating politicians (and everyone else) until nobody is left alive.

All too aware of this fact, an indigenous population will remove itself from any place conquered by zombies (or zombielike soldiers). Stop for a moment and consider what an advantage this is! If you fight like a zombie, you won't have to deal with:

- Insurgent terrorism
- Political upheaval
- Complicated plots to overthrow you
- Sycophantic flattery from sympathizers to your side (Ick, right?)

> **Don't bring a knife to a gunfight**
>
> Do, however, bring zombies to a gunfight, because once people are out of bullets, the zombies will just eat everybody.

- People throwing shoes at you during press conferences

There will be, quite simply, nobody left at all.

(**Note:** History is full of examples of defensive forces that willingly fought to the last man—even though they knew their cause could not be won—to make a glorious show of patriotism and demonstrate to the enemy the depth of their dedication to the cause. Yet **nobody** has ever elected to defend a city [or shuttered public house, or abandoned shopping mall] to the last man when it was being attacked by zombies. Coincidence? Of course not. Being insensible to things like patriotism, fidelity to one's country, and human emotions in general, zombies would not be impressed by [or even be likely to notice] a valiant human's last stand.)

So when laying siege to a city, make absolutely clear to your opponents that you intend to fight like zombies. This means that the following will happen:

Prisoners will not be taken. Everybody gets eaten (or whatever you're planning to do to them).

The institutions of the city—from its award-winning ethnic food to its internationally known opera house—will not be maintained or preserved by the occupying force once the city is conquered. Your side has no interest in taking the city just in order to post an "Open under new management!" sign out front a few weeks later. To the contrary, like a zombie, your plan will be to take what you can eat/use, and leave the rest to rot.

Your soldiers, like zombie soldiers, will not distinguish between enemy soldiers engaging them with deadly force and orphans and widows who are just there being pitiful-looking and annoying.

Truces, cease-fires to collect dead bodies, and any other mutually established cessations in combat are completely off the table. Like zombies, once your side starts bringing it, it will "be brought" until everyone is dead.

Your side will not adhere to any "conventions" during the forthcoming combat. Like zombies, you don't play by rules. (Remember: "If you can do it, **you can do it!**")

As you have no plans to occupy and keep up the city after you capture it, your disregard for its physical structures will be complete. Seeking to preserve nothing, you will burn bridges, poison wells, and knock down load-bearing walls with giant demolition balls if it suits your purposes. You will use priceless works of art to pick your teeth and culturally significant artifacts to shine your shoes. Like a zombie, you have *zero* regard for whatever you are attacking.

No record of the forthcoming battle will ever exist. (Zombies don't write shit down after they do it.) Dispel any dreams the defenders may have of making a glorious last stand "worthy of a song." (Zombies don't write songs, either.) Instead, defenders should understand that they are only worthy of being killed and/or eaten by an enemy that will forget about them completely once their brains have passed down the esophagus and into the stomach.

Finally—and most terrifyingly—make clear that you are not attacking the city because it is a strategically significant place to occupy, because you intend to use it as a staging center for additional operations, or because it will afford you a tactical advantage. Nope. The only reason you're attacking the city is because **there are a lot of people there.** You are attacking the people in the city, and not the city itself. (Cities are just handy for zombies and zombie warriors, because people tend to concentrate in them.) Make clear: You are here to kill people, not because you want the things (a city) that people have.

So issue these warnings to the place you're about to attack and see if, gee, they don't *suddenly* start acting like you're **an army of actual zombies.** When your enemy understands that things like negotiation, escape, or surrender of any kind are going to be impossible once battle is joined, you're going to see a *much* higher percentage of them (like 100 percent) quietly creeping out through the city gates before your army arrives to start the siege in earnest.

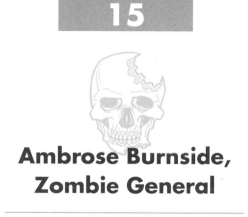

Ambrose Burnside, Zombie General

Sometimes military commanders do everything right but still come up short. They play each card correctly, yet (one must say it) fail to achieve their ultimate objectives. History records them as having been middling or ineffective leaders, when, in truth, they could not have possibly done anything more to ensure victory.

It is into this category that one must place American Civil War General Ambrose Burnside. He was a soldier, a leader, a facial-hair pioneer . . . and quite possibly the only Zombie Commander in the Grand Army of the Republic.

Burnside understood the value of attacking the enemy like a horde of zombies and exhibited this in battle after battle. A student of military history will find no finer example of his battlefield acumen on display than Burnside's operation to take the bridge over Antietam Creek—the so-called Burnside's Bridge—at the Battle of Antietam.

On September 17, 1862, Burnside, under General George B. McClellan, engaged Confederate troops at Sharpsburg, Maryland. Antietam Creek ran through tactically important portions of the battlefield, and Burnside was ordered to secure it. To do this, he knew he needed to cross it and secure both sides. Like any good Zombie Commander, Burnside thought to himself: *How can I do this in a way that involves my troops just charging straight at the enemy all goddamn day?*

Military historians are quick to criticize Burnside for neglecting to deduce that Antietam Creek was only fifty feet across at the widest point and only waist-deep. Further, they note, the Confederate forces did not monitor many sections of the creek. (The inference put forward seems to be that Burnside should have had his soldiers wade across and flank the enemy, or something boring and stupid like that.) These so-called historians fail to notice, however, Burnside's having been a zombie (which casts any positive estimation of their skill as historians into serious doubt).

No, when looking to take Antietam Creek, Burnside resolved to do it like a zombie. His keen zombie eyes surveyed the battlefield and lit upon the one piece of geography that would make this possible: the single, well-defended, narrow bridge that forded the creek. Here, Burnside understood, was an opportunity to use the terrain to make his soldiers fight like members of the walking dead.

All day, Burnside sent wave after wave of troops over the bridge in conspicuous, zombielike fashion. Yet, as the battle drew on (with what appeared—to the untrained, nonzombie eye—to be a lack of progress on Burnside's part) General McClellan began sending dispatches to Burnside. (e.g., "Why haven't you taken the creek?" "Why are you just marching men, three-abreast, across the bridge again and again, effectively negating your advantage of superior numbers?" "What's this rumor I hear about you directing our troops to eat the Confederates' brains?") Eventually, McClellan lost patience and ordered other brigades to "help" Burnside take the creek by "not just attacking over one tiny goddamn bridge."

Today, we can only imagine the resounding zombie victory Burnside would have won had his efforts not been curtailed by senior commanders who insisted in meddling with his obviously awesome battle tactics.

While, on the face of it, this support appears to have allowed Burnside to be successful in completing his assigned military objective, it also failed to end the engagement in a decisive, undead fashion. To wit: Though defeated, the Confederates defending the bridge lived to fight another day (as opposed to all being eaten).

The opposing army left the engagement with a lesson running something like: "If the Union troops are being mowed down in wave after wave, they will eventually try something else (as opposed to "The Union troops will just keep coming and coming and coming until we run out of ammo and have to use our bayonets, and even then they will keep coming." [It's like: "I don't know about you, Zeke, but I'm starting to think we should just let these guys free those slaves. They seem to really want it."])

> **War is too important to be left to the generals**
>
> Seriously. Things always go better when they're handled by a bunch of rotting reanimated corpses who are out to eat some brains. It's like: Okay Mr. General-guy, you've had your say at the press conference. Now let the experts take it from here.

Burnside was censured and accused of attacking like a complete jackass (as opposed to being given a medal for zombie awesomeness).

If McClellan and others had simply given Burnside's approach the **time it needed to work**, then the enemy would have eventually been overtaken by Burnside's shambling, hoary army of zombielike fighters. The Confederates would have soon exhausted their ammunition, succumbed to physical exhaustion, and been completely demoralized by the knowledge that they faced a foe that would continue to attack in the lockstep manner of the undead.

16

Planes, Trains, and Automobiles

Also: tanks, submarines, battleships, and up-armored Hummers with mounted machine guns. These are all things that some idiots somewhere thought could (a) destroy zombies, and/or (b) at the very least protect their occupants **from** zombies. These ideas are wrong. Beyond wrong, actually. Dangerous. Dangerous to anyone who would fight zombies.

No contraption of war so far fashioned by man has ever proved effective against zombies, at least not in any large-scale way. From the most imposing medieval siege engine to the newest modern mobile command vehicle, zombies have always found ways to get inside and utterly fuck that shit up.

Zombies have a habit of penetrating impenetrable hulls, stowing away in airplane bomb bays, and showing up inside

115

submarines just after they submerge. They render war machines useless by interacting with them **in ways you're not supposed to.** Zombies engage the enemy, all right, but not in the ways their opponents are expecting.

When a German U-boat captain opens a torpedo tube and finds himself suddenly being strangled by some kind of Nazi zombie (perhaps in a moth-eaten SS uniform), he may cry out: "You're not supposed to be in there!" But that fact isn't stopping the zombie, is it, Klaus? You're still getting strangled, aren't you?

When a Viking horde sets sail for the mainland on a mission of plunder, old Leif may be confounded by the strange moving skeleton that first appeared to be a part of the masthead, but is now moving across the deck and attacking his compatriots at the oars. The mighty Nordic warship will cease to function at all as the zombie rips through the throats of these men who cry out to "Odin," "Freya," and other asinine deities for help. Mastheads can't move? That's funny, 'cause it sure seemed like that masthead was moving a lot when it **just fucking killed you.**

When a medieval soldier riding an elephant with a mangonel mounted on it decides to use this weapon to demoralize his foe by shooting cadavers into the enemy camp, he's going to be more than a little surprised when that sack of bodies he brought along suddenly starts moving. He'll be positively astounded when zombies start ripping through the sack and coming to eat his brains. (The elephant they'll leave alone.)

But zombies do more than just fuck up and destroy these vessels of war. They also use them to move from place to place. In doing so, zombies demonstrate how a problem facing the contemporary military commander can be addressed with the help of zombies. And that problem is: **troop transport.**

From the beginning of organized warfare, soldiers have been forced to travel in all manner of uncomfortable and undignified ways. They have been forced to ride noncompliant, smelly animals and to pack themselves like sardines in uncomfortable machinery. While these modes of transportation were often unpleasant for the soldiers involved, they were even more unpleasant for the commander, who was **left with the fucking bill to pay.** Giant warships and fleets of airplanes are expensive and must be maintained. Gasoline is expensive. Pilots and drivers and captains are expensive. How often has a conventional general wished with desperate longing that his soldiers could move with the ease of zombies? (**Answer:** All the damn time.)

Zombies move on foot most of the time—and can march all night with no need to rest. Even on foot and at a relaxed pace, they can often outdistance a slower-moving motorized form of transport. But never forget that zombies can also employ mechanized or animal transport when it suits them. Zombies are the infinitely resourceful ride-hitchers of the militarized world. They have no armada of vehicles to speak of, yet always manage to use tanks, planes, and even light rail to arrive precisely when they should. How do they do this? Simple. They **adopt, adapt, and appropriate.**

First of all, a zombie's concept of what is "mine" and what is "yours" is very loose to begin with. (A zombie understands that the brain it smells is "yours" and that it wants to make it its own with all speed—but that's about as far as it goes.) When a zombie—or a group of zombies—sees a freighter docked on the coast of Haiti about to depart for the mainland, it doesn't consider the vessel's ownership as it stealthily lumbers up the gangplank and creeps into the bowels of the ship. The ship may be "yours," but the zombie is still "riding it to the Florida coast."

Zombies have no use for tickets or passports. They simply board the nearest form of transport and take it to wherever it is going.

When a zombie wants to travel (which it always does, in search of brains) it uses whatever means are handy to make that travel dream happen. But just as a lone zombie can stow away on a pleasure cruise (and then emerge from the cargo hold to fuck things up at the captain's table during dinner), so, too, can an entire battalion of zombies infiltrate an international freighter bound for foreign lands.

Remember: Those who transport zombies almost always do so unwittingly.

So then how, as a contemporary military commander, are you to harness the travel advantages of zombies? (It's not like you can have an entire army just "stow away" on a ship. . . .)

Actually, you can. While low-minded military officers (thugs, really) simply "appropriate" everything in sight (thus sowing discontent among the boat- and plane-owning populace that will eventually contribute to their own demise), sensible **zombie** officers just borrow things for a little while.

If your army needs to cross a lake and there are a bunch of boats right there, then sure, you're going to take them. Across the lake. But that's it. You're not going to steal the boats and claim them for whatever country or despot you're fighting for. No. You're going to leave them when you're done (if not returning them to the original owners). **That's** the important thing. When a zombie finds itself in the cargo deck of an airplane, the zombie's goal is not to own that airplane. The zombie is just using it temporarily to get to where it needs to go (a population center). And if it gets to chow down on an in-flight meal of stewardess with a side of baggage-handler, then so much the better.

Whether your army needs to cover a few city blocks or needs to cross entire continents, make an army of zombies and temporarily appropriate all means of travel that present themselves. Consider:

Subway cars and subway systems can be useful when transporting soldiers small distances within an urban center. If you have established yourself as a zombie army hostile to everyone, you should have no trouble convincing the indigenous commuters to wait for the 5:15 while your guys get on to go plunder the city center.

Buses and limousines are a fun way of transporting soldiers across town or on longer trips if necessary. You may have to do your own driving, but showing up for a military coup in a limo is a classy way to start your regime. (Or hey, take the bus if you'd rather be a workingman, Hugo Chávez–style insane dictator.)

Aircraft, from planes to helicopters, should be appropriated whenever your soldiers need to travel long distances or descend from the air . . . and when, you know, you're near an airport.

Submarines and ocean liners should always be employed when your army needs to travel across great distances involving water. Duh. (Some actual zombies have been known to walk around along the bottom of the ocean, but then, the sharks . . .)

So when methods of transport present themselves, go ahead and take advantage of them. When your trip is over, go on your merry way with no further thought as to the fate of these discarded vessels. Zombies look for opportunity, when it comes to traveling or otherwise. So should it be with you.

Encirclement

We've covered the advantages of Always Just Marching Straight Ahead in the direction of your enemy. One contingency to be prepared for is the result of this tactic when employed against an enemy whose troops are fewer in number and/or more tightly packed than your own. Namely, your troops will encircle your enemy.

Note that this is more than just a "side effect" of marching a bunch of soldiers (who don't want to patiently stand in line behind one another) toward a smaller encampment of enemies. It is a tactic that has been used by zombies since the beginning of time and should be adopted by you whenever possible.

In dialogues pertaining to combat, generals speak of wanting to flank and rout one another's armies but rarely of "encircling" them. This is because most generals have in mind the goal of compelling the opposing army to either run away or to surrender. Very few military leaders have the goal of "eating every last one of the enemy's brains, no matter how much time or how much effort we must expend to make that happen." (It is no coincidence that very few military leaders fight with the effectiveness and skill of zombies.)

When an army of zombies marches into battle, it does so not to "win the day" but to "eat the enemy alive." As such, a zombie army seeks to maximize the number of its troops coming into direct contact with enemy troops. If a zombie army is on the offensive (which, if it's doing things right, it should always be), it will usually find enemies in fortified positions that are nonetheless able to be encircled. This is helpful when it comes to maximizing the number of zombies that can mass along a perimeter.

When analyzing nineteenth- and twentieth-century warfare, military historians often point toward victory being determined by the side that could "throw the most lead" at the other. This means that the side that could fire the fastest while facing the enemy directly—**or while firing over obstacles**—at the enemy usually won. But zombies are decidedly short-range combatants. They can't fire over or around things. Thus, a zombie army's only real option is getting as many zombies as possible close to the enemy. Zombie armies win by maximizing the amount of teeth-on-the-line they have going at any given time. (Zombie soldiers can think of this as the ABC Principle: **Always Be Cannibalizing.**)

Say a medieval zombie army finds its opponents holed up in a palace, replete with high walls, keep, and drawbridges. Now, while a conventional fighting force might attempt to find the weakest point in the palace and focus attacks there, a zombie army will instead surround the entire palace and attack all possible points at once. Is there going to be some wasted effort? Sure. Are there going to be stone walls and iron gates impervious even to a zombie's teeth? Absolutely. Are some zombies going to get drenched with hot tar or flaming arrows—or possibly hot tar *and* flaming arrows? Yes. (Look, I'm starting to wonder whose side you're really on, here.) The point is that the zombies will attack anyone they can find at *any* point along the face of the structure. In doing so, the zombies will lower the morale of the palace's inhabitants (giving them an unpleasant "surrounded by murderous zombies" feeling), and will also allow them to explore the building's perimeter for any unprotected fissures or exploitable openings (zombies *always* find some of these).

What if your enemy is not using man-made or natural cover to protect himself? What if he has not massed his army at the top of a hill or within a fortress, but is instead waiting to engage you on the open plain? If this is the case, there should be **no adjustment** to your strategy. Run your army headlong into his. Rather than concentrating on any point in his line (or breaking your troops down into units that move in elaborately coordinated formations), have your soldiers attack horde-style by running at the enemy until they are face to face with an enemy soldier. As always, the use of cover should be eschewed. Any movement, in fact, that fails to bring your soldiers **face to face** with the legion of the enemy should be discouraged. By attacking the enemy in this fashion, your troops will eventually fan out until they create a circle around the enemy. This circle may be thin or even intermittent in places, but this should not raise concerns for you. Once an enemy is encircled—and your zombie troops are maximizing the amount of your troops coming into direct contact with their troops—you will begin to gain the upper hand.

Here's a secret: If you act as though surrender, capitulation, and flight are **not** the goals of your attack, you will often create **exactly those responses in your enemy.**

Enemy armies expect to, on some level, *understand* what an opponent wants to get out of an engagement. Usually, when they are on the defensive (which, again, they will be **because you will always be attacking**), they are trying to prevent something from happening. An enemy general will typically be thinking things like:

> "This position is ours. They want to take it, so we're gonna stop them!"

"Our unit possesses valuable matériel that the enemy would like to capture. We must defend it at all costs!"

"Our armies were destined to meet somewhere, and it looks like it will be here. Let us fight until the other surrenders or retreats!"

"The enemy wants us out of his land. Let us show them that we will not retreat or take one step backward. We are here to stay!"

These gallant and well-intentioned declamations make sense in most situations, but not when you're fighting zombies (or soldiers who fight like zombies). What the enemy commanders in these examples fail to understand is that zombies want to kill them and eat their brains. While Zombie Commanders may use zombies to further tactical and political agendas, the zombies on the ground (which is to say all of them [unless you've created some kind of flying zombie . . . which would be totally awesome]) don't care about politics or tactics. **They just want to eat you.** This fact will become crystal clear to the enemy general and his troops once you encircle them. They'll be all, "Wait a minute . . . . Something's wrong here. These guys are acting like killing machines that can't be reasoned with. And it's hard to get killing machines to capitulate, surrender, or call a truce to recover bodies of fallen comrades. Maybe I totally misunderstood what I was getting into by fighting these guys. Jesus . . . Maybe I should be pull back and reassess this opponent before more of my men get eaten. And maybe I should do it **real fucking soon**, because they seem to be forming a circle around us."

By acting as though compelling your enemy to flee the battle-field is the last thing on your mind, you will in fact make it **the first thing that he does.**

Another key advantage of encirclement, as with Always Just Marching Straight Ahead, is that it makes the enemy generals working against you second-guess the condition of their own army. While opposing commanders will try to anticipate your attack (for you **will** be the one always attacking), they will identify their own perceived weak points and expect you to strike them. Let me say that another way: **They think they already know where you'll strike.** You will, then, confound your enemy by simply attacking **everywhere, all at once, on his perimeter.** Does this mean that, in some cases, a number of your troops will have to fall in the name of attacking the enemy at his strongest, most reinforced point? Unfortunately so. But their efforts shall not have been in vain. Attacking every-where will sow doubt and confusion in the opposing general's tasty, tasty brain. He will begin to think you know something he doesn't. (In a larger sense, this will be correct; you know that fighting like a zombie is the way to win battles.) He will wonder:

> "Have I misunderstood my own most vulnerable point?"

"Have I misunderstood which of my own troops are the most valuable?"

"Have I perhaps misunderstood the tactical advantage of certain battlefield positions? We're being attacked on the higher ground affording a complete view of the battlefield, true. But we're also being attacked along the banks of that muddy creek that flows through a valley where everybody can shoot at you. Have I, in my arrogance, perhaps underestimated the value of that creek? It offers no cover, and you get stuck there, and everybody can shoot at you . . . but still, there must be a **reason** my opponent wants it. I'm getting this feeling that **we need to defend this creek at all costs!**"

But no amount of italics can adequately convey the disheartening and confusing effect that your encircling the enemy and attacking his every point will have on the situation. A zombie fights without hesitation, ceaselessly, and everywhere it can. When you attack your enemy at every point along his line, weak or strong, you will further convince your opponent that he needs to abandon his original battle plan. He may even consider leaving the field of battle until he can reconnoiter with his subordinates and try to understand what the enemy is doing.

In summary, you need to encourage your troops to encircle the enemy and attack him at all points along his line. Any short-term losses—coming, for example, by charging your soldiers into places where a bunch of giant guns are—will be recovered a hundredfold when your enemy realizes that he has no fucking clue what's going on with you. By attacking like a bunch of mindless zombies that charge blindly at the first enemy soldier they see, your attack will have an effect more powerful than the most meticulously calculated battle plan. Your enemy will flee, surrender, or get eaten (or at least killed). Whatever the case, I think it's safe to say you win.

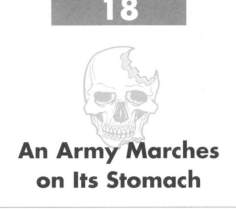

An Army Marches
on Its Stomach

An army marches on its stomach, or so runs the axiom. Zombies march to put people *in* their stomachs. Forget chow wagons and KP and peeling potatoes as punishment—a zombie's relationship between eating and fighting is much simpler. If a zombie doesn't "win" a particular combat or engagement, it doesn't eat. Period. Conversely, if a zombie does win an engagement, it "wins" all that it needs to eat.

This idea has existed as long as zombies have, and for good reason. Everybody needs to eat; this includes soldiers and *especially* includes zombie solders. Let's face it, marching and fighting and then marching again (and possibly pillaging somewhere in there, too) is hard fucking work. Your troops are going to expend a lot of calories doing your bidding, and

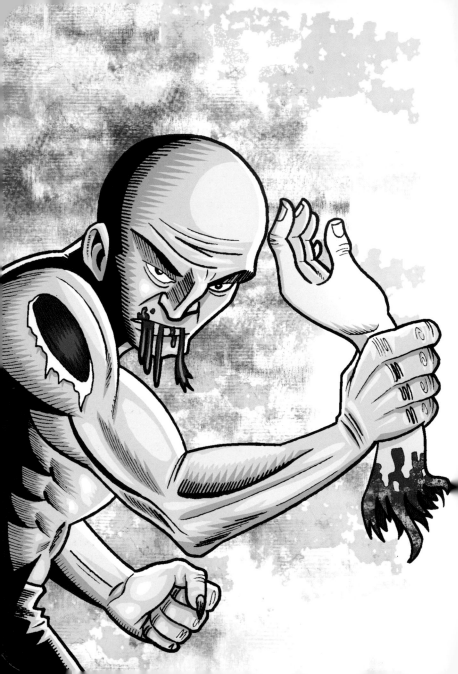

you're going to need to replenish those calories if you want to have anything resembling an effective fighting force.

Most generals have the sense to ensure that their soldiers are adequately provisioned—again, this is not a new idea, but the oldest one in the book—but few commanders think to actively encourage gluttony in the ranks. This, however, is **precisely** what you want to do if your goal is to cultivate the most effective fighting force possible. Remember, zombies are your models, and what are zombies if not consummate gluttons for brains?

Zombies don't dine on rations. They dine on you. But this is never to imply that food is not on a zombie's mind. Zombies stalk through the world driven by their hunger for the living flesh and the still-thinking brains of humans. Food is the *first* thing on a zombie's mind. Food is what drives its every lurch forward, what motivates it to ford streams, cross scalding deserts, and spend hour after tedious hour tunneling into the basement of an inner-city orphanage. "Rationing" that food would be an upsetting (and flatly unacceptable) option for a zombie.

The very word "ration" can mean to dole something out slowly so as to preserve it—which is one thing when you've got a finite amount of supplies and a battalion of hungry soldiers to feed. But if you're a horde of angry zombies, this is a different prospect entirely.

Zombies have no concept of "enough" when it comes to brains and the mayhem and murder that must be wreaked to attain them. Zombies lack the concept of "full" as you and I are able to understand the term. A zombie army's entire performance on a battlefield (or anyplace else) is entirely dictated by its collective "stomach."

There is nothing wrong with your troops hungering desperately for something, as long as you make clear that getting it involves the successful completion of a combat objective. Your soldiers might not want to eat brains, but steak and lobster shouldn't be out of the question. If you don't have the proper kitchen equipment on the battlefield for something froufrou, then at least put a pig on a spit and tap a few kegs of beer. These soldiers have been fighting all day, and now they deserve to kick back a little. Damn. Don't you think they've earned it?

So encourage your soldiers (if they be human) to expect a glorious feast at the conclusion of a battle. Have them associate victory with "getting to eat." The result will be troops who fight very much like zombies.

Know Quarter?
No! No Quarter!

(Just kill everybody.)

When a group of soldiers comes up against a zombie horde, it understands that—should the battle not go well—being taken prisoner is probably not on the table.

Zombie armies don't have POW or prisoner-exchange programs. (It would be sort of pointless to a zombie, because zombies would just eat the prisoners. Further, zombies have less than no concern for their fellow zombies. If a zombie gets captured by a group of humans, it's like: "Sorry, dude. I've got more important things to do than worry about rescuing you. Like eating people's brains.")

So zombies don't take prisoners. When that horde breaks through the trenches and spills over into your position, you can throw down your weapon and raise your hands above your

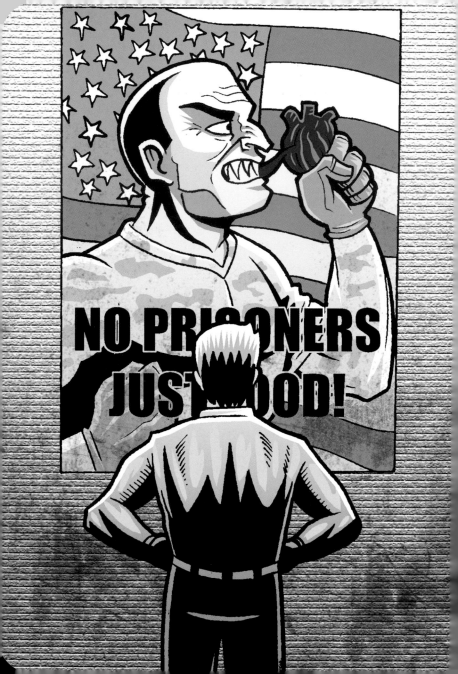

head if you want to, but the zombies are just going to keep coming, so you might as well keep shooting.

But lest you think that facing a zombie foe *inspires* soldiers to fight to the last man, please note that the fact of this lack-of-prisoner-taking is more demoralizing than any propaganda campaign.

I mean, throughout the history of war, generals have attempted to portray enemy soldiers as subhuman or less-than-human. This is perceived as conferring several advantageous qualities to their own troops, among them:

Less compunction about killing an inhuman enemy

Hatred for the enemy (in the same way your soldiers might hate the cockroaches or centipedes to which they are compared)

Less fear of the enemy (Cockroaches and centipedes might be gross and annoying, but you can just step on them, right?)

This dehumanization really hit its stride during World War II, when technology had advanced, but political correctness didn't exist yet, so you had the Golden Age of Disney and Warner Brothers cartoons (which you can now find only on YouTube) portraying entire races as subhuman or animal-like. However, these portrayals are always done in a way that makes the enemy seem contemptible or less threatening. You don't see propaganda where the enemies are made to look like unicorns or lions or some sort of kick-ass animal. That would be detrimental to the whole project. But that's exactly what you run into with zombies.

When a foe becomes something that is less-than-fully-human in an awesome or terrifying way, then suddenly its "other-ness" is no longer a military advantage.

When you're watching a horror movie, and a guy says something like: "Those things aren't human!" it's not a **good** thing. He's not *happy* that those things aren't human. Rather, it's an expression of alarm and terror.

Things that aren't human certainly aren't going to negotiate, or abide by the Geneva Convention, **or take prisoners.**

In a way, this approach to warfare ups the ante, so to speak. This approach says: "We're going to just go ahead and settle this **now.**" Opposing generals may be looking forward to—and, more importantly, planning for—a long, drawn-out conflict that will be decided over the course of many battles and campaigns, possibly spanning years. They may anticipate regular truces and negotiations between generals (probably conducted in air-conditioned, oak-paneled rooms where everybody gets a comfy chair and a tumbler of brandy). Refusing to stop to take prisoners—or for any other reason—will befuddle, upset, and generally demoralize the leadership that opposes you.

Zombies don't like long, drawn-out conflicts. They are very direct. (They'd much prefer to kill you and eat your brains right now, thank you very much.) And while zombies have—usually against their collective will—sometimes become involved in lengthy standoffs outside malls or firearms stores, they'd prefer to settle things ASAP. No prisoners. No negotiations. No questions asked.

When you become a general who refuses to take prisoners, your reputation will precede you into battle. Enemies facing you will understand that no quarter will be asked or granted, and that your troops are ready to fight to the last. (Not that we want it coming to that, obviously.)

While all warfare is deadly, you just found a way to make it deadlier for everyone involved. Congratulations, dude. Now you're fighting like a zombie.

20

Make All Your Troops Identical and Interchangeable

How many times have you been in a combat situation—or (let's be honest here) seen a war movie—where a nervous-looking aide has had to inform a general: "Sir, we just lost artillery!" (The grizzled general then curses and slams his fist into the map laid out before him, indicating that his forces will be greatly inconvenienced by this development.)

That situation would never happen in a zombie army. Never. Why? Because in a zombie army, all of the troops are (or can be) artillery. And all of the troops are infantry. And all of the troops are amphibious assault experts.

Zombie soldiers are all these things at the same time.

They are **interchangeable.**

This is something that Zombie Commanders have long known and always used to their advantage. It's a simple idea: what one zombie can do, another can probably do, too. (It's not like zombies' special skills are divided into teams. There's not one group that can hold its breath forever, another that can withstand bullets to the torso, and yet another that can bite through a human skull like it was made out of little more than papier-mâché. **All** zombies can do **all** these things, **at all times.**)

Now, none of this is to say that zombies don't sometimes specialize. Smaller zombies can fit through cracks and fissures that hold back larger ones. Heavier zombies can walk underwater and make amphibious assaults. Zombies that can still "pass" as living humans can creep close to a human enemy before launching a "surprise" attack at close range. A zombie horde is a dynamic collection of variety, ready at all times to kill you in any number of ways.

But the most crucial aspects of zombie warfare are shared by **all** zombies. All zombies can charge an enemy with infinite bravery. All zombies can throw themselves against locked doors and barricades for hour after hour with infinite devotion and intensity. All zombies can brave fire, ice, water, and the cold soulless vacuum of outer space. In central, important ways, all zombies find a way to play a part.

So what does this mean for you? What does this mean in terms of practical steps for the would-be Zombie Commander? Certainly not "no specialization." Specialties are clearly required in most modern military situations. Instead, zombie soldiers should be trained in as many battlefield tactics as possible.

Can one soldier simultaneously be a paratrooper, a radioman, and a loader in a tank? Absolutely, if you train him to. And hey, I'm not saying they have to be the best at everything. You know that old saying, "Jack of all trades, master of none"? Well that's worked out just fine for zombies. Zombies have rotting, undead fingers—digits too swollen or rotted away to operate equipment or weapons with any kind of "mastery"—but that doesn't mean they don't still get the job done.

So familiarize your troops with as many potential battlefield eventualities as you can. You don't want your tank commander to be flopping around like a fish out of water when he's not in his tank, do you? Make him jump out of some planes. Send him on some amphibious assault training missions, and make sure he can use a rocket launcher. He doesn't have to be awesome at all of these things, but when troops become interchangeable, you can attack your enemies with the dynamism and verve of a zombie horde. And that's a **very** good thing.

21

Zombie Formation(s)

While the study of famous military engagements is an important part of any leader's training, a good general never assumes that any battle he's about to participate in will be precisely like one he's read about in a book. Every engagement is different. Every battle contains elements of the unexpected. Each battle is unique.

A Zombie Commander, however, can expect fewer surprises than a typical general, because, in a way, he has fewer options. His troops cannot retreat. They cannot be frightened. They cannot stop attacking for any reason.

For these reasons, a Zombie Commander can dispense with the traditional troop formations employed by typical generals. In fact, **he really just needs one.**

Zombies attack by charging straight at their targets, accosting them as one single force to be reckoned with, without hesitation or pacing. There is no "coordination" (strictly speaking) of what is happening. The zombies are just coming for you. (Duh.)

This formation—if it is a formation at all—might be fairly called the Marauding Horde. It can confound enemy soldiers in a number of helpful ways.

"Where are the weak points? How can we hit 'em where it hurts?"

*I dunno, sir. It's a giant mob, and they're **all** zombies. The whole mob is. And they all look about the same—like they're basically interchangeable. Attacking it in one area is pretty much going to have the same effect as attacking it in another.*

"What kind of strategy is the enemy general employing?"

Errr, "zombie strategy"? I mean, I don't think these things are "thinking" in the same way that our soldiers are. This is utterly alien and strange. We've never seen this before.

"How do we fight them?"

Ummm . . . Funny thing about that. See, nobody has ever really defeated a group of zombies so there's not any precedent for what to do here. We can meet them head-on. We can attack from all sides at once. Or we could just wait to see what they do. But it doesn't appear like we have long to make up our minds. Take a look. They're comin'.

The Marauding Horde moves forward toward an enemy like water running downhill. They squeeze into crevasses and cracks. They pursue any opening that presents itself. They will cross minefields and trenches with no hesitation. Whatever way the battlefield presents a pathway toward physical contact with an enemy, the Marauding Horde of zombies will take it.

An enemy defending a fortified position may foolishly "count on" certain defensive emplacements to stymie or slow attacking soldiers. They'll be **totally wrong**, however, when you attack as a Marauding Horde. It won't hesitate to cross a minefield. It won't slow down while crossing barbed wire to ensure that hunks of flesh aren't torn from its soldiers' bodies. Patches of flaming oil aren't going to cause your zombies to think about changing formation.

In short, attacking as a Marauding Horde will keep your assaults from being predictable and will get your troops close to the enemy as quickly as possible. When you charge as a group of zombies, your foes will soon realize that they have no clue how to fight you. Their playbook will have to go right out the window. For example, you can't really flank an attacking group of zombies, because once you start moving toward zombies, they will start moving toward you. Zombies don't stay in one place to fight. They move. Toward you.

You can't shell a group of zombies until they retreat because (for the tenth time) zombies don't retreat.

Most importantly, when facing a Marauding Horde led by a Zombie Commander, you can't study previous battles that he has fought. There will be **no way** to predict what a zombie army will do based on past efforts, because Marauding Hordes don't react to you like thinking, human soldiers who are trying not to die. Zombies might crawl through a stinking, dangerous sewer system to attack you from below. They might cross blazing, insufferable deserts for days to attack you from the least expected position possible. They may rise from an ancient, crumbling druid cemetery at the center of your army's formation, though they know full well they will be starting the battle **surrounded.**

To give your troops the effectiveness of zombies, don't spend time practicing specific formations. Instead, **let your troops make it up on their own as they charge.** (I know, encouraging soldiers to do the thinking for you is not typically how commanders stay employed, but bear with me here.) If they're properly trained as zombie soldiers, their zeal to reach the enemy will almost certainly result in a de facto Marauding Horde formation each time. Yes, there may be small variations between "Horde," "Mob," and "Amorphous Wall of Gibbering Flesh" but any zombie formation your soldiers can form will stymie your enemy equally well.

Next, use your Marauding Horde to strike in counterintuitive ways. Zombie troops don't mind being wet or hot or cold. They don't mind danger. They fight like they're already dead. If the most direct way toward the enemy camp is across a windy, ice-encrusted plateau, fraught with peril and booby traps, then that's the way they're going to go.

Enemy generals seldom expect the Marauding Horde formation that just comes out of nowhere, teeth and claws gnashing (or guns blazing). The first time they see it, they may attribute more intentionality to it than exists, which further bolsters your chances of victory. Conventional wisdom will tell your opponent: "Soldiers don't just charge in all willy-nilly. This has got to be part of some larger plan." Your opponent will begin to wonder if this attack is just a distraction, if a second surprise attack of some sort is going to follow. This confusion will allow your troops to charge in, even more crazily and bloodthirstily, and get the job done.

Sometimes, cultivating a general zombie-style disorder in your troops can be a challenge. Soldiers (like most people) naturally tend toward symmetry, and if they have a background in traditional military tactics, they will have been ordered countless times to "line up" and to "march single file" and "stay together" while operating as a unit. If you want them to fight like zombies, you're going to have to start issuing commands like "get separated" and "drift apart" and "don't catch up to everybody else." Encourage them to fall out of line, eschew coordinated movement, and attack the enemy at their own zombified pace.

In conclusion, there's just one zombie formation—the Marauding Horde. Learn to use it, and your enemies will be confused. **Then they will be dead.**

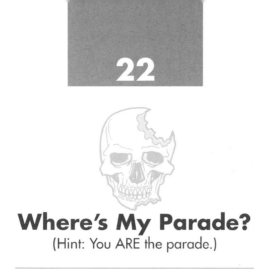

Where's My Parade?

(Hint: You ARE the parade.)

Okay, if you're a leader of actual zombies, then you probably don't expect the kingdoms you raze or the countries you conquer to throw a parade thanking you for decimating their populace and ruining their economy, infrastructure, and commerce. (In my experience, most people who start actual zombie armies aren't doing so to engender public goodwill toward themselves. Revenge and megalomania seem to be the most common motivations . . . but hey, I'm not here to judge.) But say you're just a general who has used this book to cultivate zombielike troops. Say you've used them to overthrow dictators, remove despots, and cultivate democracies in places that don't want them. "Shouldn't I," you might say, "receive **some** sort of reward? I mean, sure, my soldiers acted like zombies, but in a good way! And at the very least, we should

be acknowledged for having kicked a remarkable amount of ass on the battlefield. That counts for something, right?"

My friend, you're about to realize that not everyone is as enlightened as you or me. Many people consider acting like zombies (even in as savage a place as the battlefield) as "unconscionable," "despicable," or at least "really gross." This prejudice is deep-seated and unlikely to be dispelled by even the most decisive of military victories.

But here's the thing. Zombie soldiers can fight for a cause, a beneficent freedom fighter, or an unholy dark overlord. Or just because they're feeling hungry (brains). But zombies **don't fight to get a parade.** The bestowing of external honors on zombies is a meaningless and empty gesture. You might as well hang a medal on a dog or have a ceremony to honor a cannon.

Zombies (and troops fighting like zombies) are successful precisely because they **don't** have thoughts like: "Is fighting this battle—in this way, with these tactics—gonna get me a nice big parade when I get home?" Nope. Zombies win battle after battle because they instead think things like: "brains" and "more brains."

You've got to be honest with yourself here. Are you the kind of person who wants to win military engagements so you can marshal parades, receive decorations from dignitaries, and parlay your accomplishments into a career in politics (or at least a recurring spot on a television political discussion program)? If you are, then, gee, there are conventional armies all over the world who would love to have you and your services, but a zombie army might not be right for you.

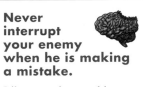

Never interrupt your enemy when he is making a mistake.

Like assuming zombies can be reasoned with. Or, ooh, assuming you can surrender to them. That's one of my favorites, too.

It's a trade-off, you see? If you command an army of zombies, you will pack an unbeatable punch on the battlefield and bring kings and tyrants to their knees . . . but you won't get celebrated for it. (Again, the prejudice against zombies just runs too deep.) Have you ever walked around a European capital and seen zombies immortalized in bronze in the city's squares? (If the zombie's arms are raised in the air, that means it died in battle, right? Or wait, maybe it's one arm. . . .) In America, where historical markers and placards dot the countryside, have you ever seen signs demarcating the locations of zombie victories? Are the accomplishments of zombie generals mentioned alongside those of Bonaparte and Wellington or Grant and Lee? The world may commemorate the accomplishments of soldiers on D-Day, but where is the Z-Day celebration?

Friend, it does not exist, nor will it ever.

People just **don't appreciate** the remarkable military accomplishments of zombies. Never mind that zombies have overthrown regimes, conquered kingdoms, and ensured that great swaths of countryside were no longer contaminated by "living things." Never mind that zombies have triumphed despite overwhelming odds, time and again. Never mind that zombies have prevailed against foes that held advantages of number, superior technology, and tactical advantage. For these remarkable accomplishments, zombies have never been rewarded or commemorated. **Nor will they ever be.**

You must not allow this fact to trouble you. Instead, you must show strength. A weaker leader—unsure of himself and his cause—is troubled by the idea that history will not record his victories, but a true Zombie Commander understands that no amount of public celebration or posthumous acclaim is worth fighting in a way that does not involve zombies.

Do you want fame, or do you want to win? That is your question.

Your answer is zombies.

Sima Yi, Zombie Commander

If there's one historical figure for whom the slogan "Just do it" came too late, it is the mysteriously zombie-like general Sima Yi, who commanded troops in China's Three Kingdoms era around the year 200. The period in Chinese history when it seemed like everybody was attacking everybody—and military leaders trying to make names for themselves were a yuan a dozen—Sima Yi was able to establish himself as one of the most feared badasses on the block by attacking his opponents in unexpected, innovative, and highly effective ways. In almost everything he did, Sima Yi employed a zombie's determination and fortitude.

Though probably not **technically** an actual zombie (as far as we know . . . records from 200 aren't the clearest), Sima Yi fought in ways that gave his troops many of the advantages enjoyed by actual zombie armies today.

Consider the following:

He was "unpredictable."

Sima Yi was known not only as a fierce fighter but also as a foe whose next move could not be easily guessed. This lack of predictability was a vexation for his enemies, who had a difficult time anticipating where he would strike next. He sometimes sent his enemies notes suggesting he would do one thing, then made a point of doing the other. Sima Yi became known in ancient China as an expert strategist precisely because his next move could so infrequently be determined in advance. But (here's the funny thing) when you look at what he actually did, it was just "attack, attack, attack." In almost every situation, Sima Yi's enemies would have best served themselves by anticipating an offensive.

Sima Yi almost just always attacked but allowed his foes to think he was likely to do otherwise. **Very like a zombie.**

He did things you "can't" do.

There are rules by which all combatants on the battlefield are bound. Ironclad rules. Rules steeped in tradition and history. Rules that cannot be broken . . . until someone wises up and just says, "Oh, wait. *Yes they fucking can!*" Sima Yi seems to have invented this.

In one of his first campaigns—at the Battle of Xincheng in 227—Sima Yi's enemies believed that he "couldn't" attack them prior to obtaining permission from the royal court, which they knew he did not have. However, Sima Yi (brilliant tactician that he was) noticed that this injunction against beginning the offensive without permission was really just **an abstract idea**, whereas his soldiers and war equipment were, quite to the contrary, **real and tactile** and perfectly arranged to attack the enemy, like, right now, without any waiting. Thus, before his opponents had time to say: "Wait a minute, you can't do tha—" Sima Yi had done it and won the battle with a swift offensive against an enemy that thought itself unable to be engaged by virtue of court doctrine.

Zombies, like Sima Yi, have won countless battles by doing things you "can't" do. They're old chestnuts by now, but how many times have we heard the following:

You can't survive multiple .38 shots to the heart.

You can't function as a military unit in environments without oxygen or sunlight.

You can't capture a fortified position if the defenders outnumber you.

You can't subsist on a diet entirely comprised of living human brain tissue. (You probably need, like, vegetables and stuff. . . .)

Except zombies **can.** And they **do.**

Zombies abide by no military conventions. (Hell, the bacteria saturating their own bodies is usually enough to qualify as "using biological weapons.") They respect no borders or boundaries or treaties. And they **certainly** don't wait for permission from a royal court before engaging an enemy. Zombies do what they do, and fuck your rules.

The longer it takes you to wake up and realize this, the longer zombies (and commanders like Sima Yi) are going to have an advantage over you.

He resisted provocation.

At the Battle of Wuzhang Plains in 234, Sima Yi faced a fierce opposing general named Zhuge Liang. Considered by many to be Sima Yi's nemesis, Zhuge Liang was also a brilliant battlefield tactician. However, as history shows, Zhuge Liang also wasn't above a bit of schoolyard name-calling. As the two opposing armies stared one another down, Zhuge Liang grew anxious and had a suit of women's clothes sent to Sima Yi, effectively calling him a girl for failing to attack fast enough. There may be no modern-day equivalent to the depth of this insult. Accounts tell us that Sima Yi's lieutenants were incensed and called for an immediate attack to punish Zhuge Liang for this intolerable gesture.

Instead, Sima Yi made the greatest tactical move of all. He did not quicken his pace at all.

Just like a zombie.

Zombies don't respond to insults or taunts. You can't bait a zombie with words (though human brains are another matter entirely). You can't hurt their feelings by pointing out short-comings. For all of their rotting, limbless decrepitude, zombies couldn't care less about the way they appear. There are no aspects of their appearance about which zombies are sensi-tive. In fact, there is **nothing** that can be said (or otherwise conveyed) to hasten a zombie's murderous, ravenous ire.

When a zombie is ready to attack you, you'll know, **because you'll be getting attacked.** (Until then, you're just going to have to sit tight.) This tendency allows zombies to triumph in many battlefield situations where those with hotter blood (or blood at all) would see a commander provoked into missteps, lured across minefields or into ambushes, or prompted to engage an enemy before he was 100 percent prepared. Zombies are never lured into traps. They are never incited to attack when the situation doesn't warrant an offensive. They never overstep their operation's objectives by fighting for things like "honor" or "pride" or "something other than brains."

By remaining unmoved by what was—in his day, at least—the biggest insult anybody had ever seen, Sima Yi displayed a zombie's fortitude and restraint, and never allowed his enemy to prompt him into joining battle before he was good and ready.

He used physical oddities to his advantage.

As is well documented, Sima Yi could turn his head around a full 180 degrees without moving the rest of his body. (Think about that for a second. Freaky, huh?) Now, we have no way of knowing how Sima Yi *felt* about this quality that made him different from other men. Perhaps he was tempted to conceal his difference from the rest of the world.

But if he *was* tempted, he didn't give in. Instead, he said, "Fuck that; I'm going to be the best turning-my-head-180-degrees general there is!" And he **was**—using his neck-turning ability on the battlefield in full view of friend and foe alike.

There is some evidence that Sima Yi's allies even derived a morale boost from this feature. (Upon seeing this physical oddity, the general Cao Cao is said to have remarked, "This guy can totally see from all directions, which will probably help out on the battlefield or something. And also: Holy shit!")

Now, everyone knows that zombies tend to have physical "differences" that—at least on the surface—separate them from normal soldiers and/or military commanders. Zombies are frequently missing limbs or eyeballs. Zombies' bodies have usually been horribly contorted and warped from years spent rotting in charnel earth or moldering at the bottom of a well. Zombies' skins have usually turned an unhealthy shade of white (which makes for really lousy camouflage unless you're in the arctic), or a disgusting greenish brown (which is sorta good for camouflage, actually).

Everyone also knows that zombies never let their physical differences stop them. They never try to hide the things that identify them as being unlike most people. They don't don makeup and wigs in an attempt to "pass" as humans. They don't attempt to "stand up straight" when their rotted spine compels them to lean forward awkwardly.

Yet this refusal to bend to the expectations of others is more than an acceptance of themselves as just the way God (or a voodoo priest or an evil wizard or secret government super-soldier project gone horribly, horribly wrong) made them. Zombies have realized that in many cases, their "differences" translate to "advantages" on the battlefield.

Zombies that lack body parts (or parts of body parts) can frequently squeeze through battlefield impediments that would stop a normal-sized soldier. Zombies can use their inability to respirate to ford deep rivers and withstand poison gas attacks. Zombies with gaping holes in their torsos can sometimes have projectile attacks pass completely through their bodies. And, yes, some zombies with especially loose spinal cords and vertebrae can swivel their heads around 180 (or even 360) degrees.

Zombies are dynamic, inventive warriors. Whenever they find a way that they are different from their opponents, they ask (or groan): "How can I use this to my advantage on the battlefield?"

The only thing he feared was the living dead.

For all the tales of derring-do and famous aphorisms attributed to Sima Yi, the utterance for which he is best remembered might be: "I can do battle with the living, but not the dead." He made this famous statement in one of the only situations where he is recorded to have run from a battlefield in cowardly terror.

But he had a good reason. (The best, really.)

The story runs that after Sima Yi's nemesis Zhuge Liang died (of natural causes [wuss]), Sima Yi brought his army to bear on Yang Yi, Zhuge Liang's successor. However, as the two generals engaged their forces, Sima Yi caught word that Zhuge Liang was not actually dead. Or that he had been dead, but now no longer was. Or that he was dead *but somehow had still been seen walking around.*

Though historians of the time do not record him using the Z-word, Sima Yi wisely decided that if these reports even had a *chance* of being true, he did not want to risk engaging an undead enemy. Instead of taking the risk that he would have to fight an actual zombie, Sima Yi wisely disengaged his army. When asked about this uncharacteristic retreat, he uttered the aforementioned quote by way of explanation.

Fearing zombies didn't really make Sima Yi *like* a zombie (or Zombie Commander). It just shows that he was smart and knew what was up. Even though the rumors about Zhuge Liang turned out to be false (he was still dead), Sima Yi gets credit for not even risking that shit and erring on the side of caution, which is always the best thing to do when it comes to zombies.

In conclusion, if you make Sima Yi your model, you'll be well on your way to becoming a Zombie Commander. Like you, Sima Yi was merely human, but he elevated himself to greatness by fighting his enemies (and winning) with the tactics of the living dead. And hey, that's all I ask.

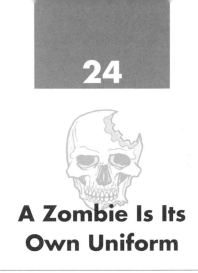

A Zombie Is Its Own Uniform

"It don't matter where you're from.
What matters is your uniform."
—Pete Townshend

Aging British rock musicians don't usually provide much in the way of useful military aphorisms, but Pete has a good point here. Uniforms are necessary for every fighting force. They engender camaraderie and teamwork, and make sure you don't shoot people on your own side.

"But wait a minute," I can already hear you saying. "Zombies don't have uniforms. Zombies are just a bunch of murderous reanimated corpses."

Exactly. And they "wear" this fact in a way that's as visible and tactile as any chevroned jacket or festooned cap.

Zombies wear the empty-eyed look of the undead—the look of those that have seen into the abyss of the grave, into the forever-blackness of the eternal. And also seen people they want to eat. Zombies are mottled and dappled with blood and entrails—sometimes their own, sometimes those of their victims—in the way a general is dappled with ribbons and medals. Zombies wear a range of physiological oddities and deformities. Zombies with bodies prepared for funeral enjoy the pasty-white sheen of the embalmed. Zombies who died in industrial accidents may still bear the Phineas Gage spikes upon which they were impaled, or at least evidence of the blunt trauma that crushed them. Zombies that were the victims of murder can crawl forth along New Jersey coasts, still dragging the "concrete shoes" or sack full of barbells with which they were buried. Zombies that have had to fight their way out of wooden caskets may be an ugly mass of splinters and wooden spikes by the time they make their way up to the sunlight. And while some zombies' bodies may have been perfumed and washed as preparation for burial (or even hollowed out with organs placed into Canopic jars), after a while, **all** zombies start to smell bad.

These qualities might not be *exactly* the same as a neatly pressed pair of parade dress slacks, but darn if they don't get the same point across.

Why am I so certain that zombies' "uniforms" are so awesome?

Zombies display **perfect** teamwork.

Zombies **never** attack other zombies.

Think about it. Have you ever heard of a zombie that wasn't "playing along"? Or a zombie that made things more difficult for his compatriots? No, you haven't. Zombies are all on the same team. (It may be the worm-eaten, maggot-infested team, but still. . . .)

And no zombie, in the history of zombies, has ever attacked another zombie. Period. This goes for on and off the battlefield. Sure, there are no extant examples of "friendly fire" among zombies (or "friendly brain-eating" if you prefer), but there are **also** no instances of zombies failing to get along before and after the carnage. There are no cases of hazing or infighting in zombie armies. No zombie in the history of the world has ever been hostile to another zombie because of religion, race, class, or ethnic background.

Thus, if you're looking to inspire troops to work with one another and treat their fellow soldiers like brothers, then let it be their dedication to fight like a zombie that creates this connection. For your ideal soldier, let there be no concern over what color he wears, the shape of his helmet (if he wears one at all), or the shine of his boots. Rather, it will be the larger, less-tangible commonalities he shares with his brothers and sisters as he lurches forward toward the enemy that will *really* allow him to be part of a successful fighting force.

A zombie is its own uniform. A zombie inspires terror and respect and can be readily identified on the battlefield. A zombie already has all of the positive qualities a uniform could lend it. Plus, if you took a bunch of perfectly good zombies, dressed them in neatly pressed combat fatigues, and marched them toward your enemy's position, it might take a while for your troops to be recognized as zombies. They might simply appear to be regular soldiers who'd had a few too many drinks the night before and were moving slowly and unsteadily as a consequence. You would lose the slow, building terror that only a group of hostile approaching zombies could conjure. (True, there would be that one moment where the zombies get close enough to be revealed for what they are, and the enemy soldiers start screaming things like: "Holy shit, they're zombies!" But tactically speaking—though it might be amusing—it isn't worth the trade-off.)

Even a small child can identify zombies from a group also containing "regular people" even though those zombies will be wearing the same coats and ties, dresses and shoes, top hats and tails as the living humans. A zombie's uniform is its posture and physical comportment, not the clothes it wears.

In conclusion, when ranging your own fighting force and preparing it for battle, you should attend to your soldiers' **uniforms**, but not necessarily to their **clothing.** Accent the defining features that they have in common, and it will accentuate their performance on the battlefield and solidify positive morale within the ranks. (And also, yeah, it'll probably help make sure they don't shoot each other, too.)

25

Behind Enemy Lines

A wonderful thing about zombies (and zombie soldiers) is their ability to function autonomously. They require a minimum of instruction to create the kind of destruction (or distraction) that you need to foil the plans of your enemy. When you send zombies behind enemy lines, you don't need to give them special intelligence briefings or covert actions trainings. You can just trust zombies to do what comes (un)naturally and rest assured that the desired effect will be achieved.

And that effect is complete and total mayhem.

It's one thing when your enemy commander has to shore up his defenses against zombie attack from a single position, but when zombies appear to have (or actually have) infiltrated from all sides and directions, his troops are likely to be unnerved and confused. There's nothing worse for an enemy soldier preparing to fight an army of zombies than being attacked from behind by zombies he did not expect to see. It matters not if these zombies make a substantive dent in the enemy's forces. Their mere **presence** will be enough to send waves of terror through the soldiers you are fighting and render them alarmed and unsure of themselves. (When fighting zombies, the only comfort one can have—if, indeed, it can be called a "comfort"—is knowing **where** the zombies are. "They are over **there**, and we are over **here.** When they come at us, we're going to shoot them down. That's how it's going to work. They're just zombies, and they're way over there. No way are we going to fuck this up." But when zombies then unexpectedly pop up behind you—*Bam!*—the whole battle plan's not so cut and dried, is it, Mr. Tough Guy?)

Nothing sends the message to your enemy that he has not fully understood the situation on the battlefield—a tactician's greatest sin—like zombies unexpectedly tapping their rear guard on the shoulder and eating their brains. When your enemy experiences this, he may be confused as to where your forces are and how they plan to attack. When this happens, you have already won 90 percent of the battle.

Thankfully, zombie-delivery systems abound. Whatever your military situation, there's usually a way to get zombies behind your enemy's lines. You can put zombies in gliders and crash-land them at your opponent's rear. You can drop them out of low-flying aircraft. You can wrangle them into catapults and

---

"Don't fire until you see the whites of their eyes."

This is something you might hear your enemies declaim as you close in on them (especially if they are using short-range flintlock musketry). The thing is, many zombies lack eyes entirely. Those that do still have eyes have often had them turn unusual colors. (Blood-red and sickly yellow are popular, for example). The point is that this should be enough to fluster and confuse enemy soldiers who are trying to obey orders. By the time they do notice that, hey, your eyes are all kinds of crazy colors but not white, your guys will be closing in to eat their brains.

---

launch them behind the walls of a hostile castle. You can pile them into a rocket and launch the rocket into your enemy's trenches. Maybe a couple of the zombies will be irreparably damaged on impact, but at least a few are bound to crawl out of the smoking crater intact enough to start some shit. (If you're dealing with zombie-like troops who are not actual zombies, you may need to employ more subtlety in your deployment. Things like parachutes and seat belts may be called for.)

Apply zombies in this fashion as liberally as possible, and as frequently as needed.

If you're involved in an extended campaign with complicated, ever-changing battle lines, it may behoove you to send a constant stream of zombies behind enemy lines at as many points as you like. If you oppose an enemy army that has fanned out across wooded terrain, deploy a detachment of zombies to the far side of those woods. If your enemy is isolated in a single, hard-to-reach point—like a castle on top of a mountain—find a way to sprinkle zombies down on top of him.

Remember, your goal is not to defeat the enemy army with these detachments. Rather, your goal is to unnerve and confuse your enemy so completely that he fails to defend himself when you attack in earnest with the bulk of your army. Don't worry that these behind-the-lines deployments may not be tactically advantageous or even sensible. You're not encircling your enemies in order to attack them from all points. At this point, you're just scaring them (so that when you **do** attack and encircle them it will be devastating and confusing).

Also, be sure to stress to your zombie troops who volunteer (or, depending on your leadership style, "volunteer") for this assignment that it's not a suicide mission. (As discussed previously, suicide missions are something that zombies **don't** do.) You're not deploying them behind the lines to pick fights they can't win. They are to engage the enemy as the opportunity presents itself **and in such a way as to make their presence known.** That's all.

If you have humans, encourage your troops to attack the enemy and then shrink back soundlessly into the underbrush. Dispatch a few enemy soldiers and leave their bodies in a conspicuous place (possibly with the brains eaten) for the others to find. Sometimes, less is more when it comes to creating uneasiness. A mere group of zombies ominously silhouetted against a sunset **in a place where they should not be** can be more effective at demoralizing the enemy than any attack or loss of life.

Generally, zombies can be counted on to do all of these things (and more!) just by being themselves. Your only concern—as a commander—will be the timing. You want to position your units behind the line so they're noticed by the enemy at the optimum time. Usually, this will be just before you attack with the bulk of your forces.

If you've deployed your behind-the-lines zombies properly, your assault (frontal and stumbling and slow as it may be) will enjoy the ease and facility of a surprise attack because your enemy will have become unsure of himself. In such a situation—and not coincidentally because they are **always** sure of themselves   zombie soldiers will certainly triumph.

Decoration
(Desecration!)

The Medal of Honor.

The Order of Victory.

The Iron Cross.

These and similar commendations have been given to soldiers of the modern era to recognize the greatest acts of heroism and gallantry on the battlefield. They single out soldiers for specific acts and acknowledge them with a physical manifestation of their nation's gratitude (usually, a medal) that can be worn so that others are instantly alerted to that soldier's accomplishments.

Zombies are never recognized by governments for their accomplishments on the battlefield, even really impressive ones. When zombies *do* manage to become "different" or "singled-out" for having done something totally awesome, it is not effected through a congressional act or dictatorial decree. Rather, it is **through the actions of the zombies themselves** that an external notice of their accomplishment comes into being.

If a zombie breaks through a barricade that no other zombie has ever been able to crack (thereby providing access to a trove of delicious humans for the rest of the army), then this zombie will likely be "rewarded" with hands and a face encrusted with splinters and scars from the tearing and destruction involved. This tells the other zombies (and humans, too) that, hey, **this** zombie means business.

When a zombie bravely walks across a fire pit to feast on cowering humans huddling on the other side, that zombie's skin may be seared forever to a blackened crisp (or may fall away entirely, revealing an anatomy model of muscles and sinew). For the rest of its days, that zombie will bear the marks of its triumphant (and entirely literal) trial by fire.

A zombie that takes out a human sniper (who has been decimating an army of zombies from a bird's nest) is going to have to climb the stairs of the clock tower, break down the door, and surprise the sniper from behind. Even if the zombie does this successfully, the sniper is still likely to get a few surprised shots off before having his brain eaten. These glistening lead "decorations" will attest to the zombie's heroism in ways that no manufactured trophies could.

Soldiers' actions create their own tokens of acknowledgment. **This is not a new idea.**

In the Gettysburg Address, President Abraham Lincoln spoke about his "poor power to add or detract" from the heroism of the men who had fought there. Old Abe had a good point. Someone who does something heroic and then has a medal pinned to his/her/its chest does not become more heroic **because of the medal.** It was, you know, the heroic thing they did.

Listen to Lincoln, and let the scars of battle themselves be the only thing that "consecrates" (to use his words) a soldier as heroic or brave. Let your zombie troops or actual zombies wear their scars and injuries as their totems of triumph. Don't have ceremonies in which soldiers are decorated with medals. Don't dapple your troops in gold and silver. Instead, allow them to wear their wounds as proudly as any medal. Attention should be drawn to their battle scars. For example, patches should never be used to obscure the sight of an eye lost in battle. Clothes should be rent so that festering bullet holes and deep stab wounds are visible to all. (Yeah, it might be a little gross or whatever, but suck it up, dude. We're fighting a war here.)

Remember: Encourage your troops to fight bravely and kill the enemy in heroic ways, but don't then get all arrogant and full of yourself and be like, "Now, brave soldier, I have the power to bestow heroism upon you with this tiny gold disk tethered to a suspiciously flamboyant-looking ribbon."

It's like, what the hell? **You** aren't making the soldier heroic. He **already was.**

Note: History records revealed that some generals made a point of rewarding soldiers who were wounded in the front but not soldiers who were wounded in the back. The implication was that soldiers wounded in the back were running away at the time when they were injured. This policy not only produced some false positives and false negatives—like soldiers who turned to run but ran into a bayonet or something—but also promulgated the practice of a general acting as some kind of heroism arbiter after the fact. Remind **your** soldiers that wherever they are wounded, it is up to their own consciences (and their wounds themselves) to determine if their actions have been adequately heroic. Make it clear that you intend to have no say in the matter.

Fast-Moving? Slow-Moving? You Need Both!

How can we be lovers if we can't be friends? How can we make love if we can't make amends? And how can we unite in eldritch murderousness to feast on the flesh of the living if we spend all of our time bickering over whether "fast zombies" or "slow zombies" are better?

Seriously. This debate needs to end now.

Both kinds of zombies are totally awesome, totally deadly, and totally able to coexist in a military unity. I mean, if these zombies can accept their own differences, why can't *we*?

Let's be honest, the most hackle-raising part of this debate comes from fast zombies. It starts there. At first, zombies were just slow. They were slow physically and mentally. They

stumbled into things. They got confused. They often walked with arms outstretched like sleepwalkers. But then fast zombies started showing up. They wanted to eat your brain and drink your blood, but they also wanted to win the hundred-yard dash. They sprinted after their prey like a pack of wolves. Some observers regarded them as an "innovation" or "improvement" on the original, slow-moving zombies. Others regarded them as "not fucking zombies because they run."

While death is seldom understood to endow superpowers, it does appear to have granted *some* zombies tremendous speed. This is a fact we all have to suck up and face. Does it follow that these zombies should be ostracized or eliminated entirely from your zombie army? **By no means.** Both fast and slow zombies have military advantages. The master zombie tactician will use them in symphony to crush and fluster the enemy. In fact, an army composed of equal parts fast and slow zombies will have advantages over a group composed solely of either. Consider these scenarios:

Storming a castle

Fast zombies will attempt a frontal assault, much like human soldiers (and, like them, will be subjected to hot oil that will boil their tendons apart, fire weapons designed to disintegrate them, and moats that sink [or at least slow] them). In a best-case scenario, flaming, oily zombies jump the moat and slither under the portcullis.

Slow zombies will gradually gather around the castle's outermost fortifications and knock around against it like a bunch of lost pinballs. They will be able to sense humans inside the castle wall, but

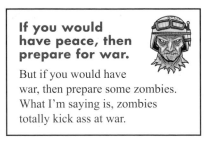

If you would have peace, then prepare for war.

But if you would have war, then prepare some zombies. What I'm saying is, zombies totally kick ass at war.

will have no quick way to get at them. A best bet for victory is for zombies to starve out the humans (until they decide they have to make a break for it), but that may take many days.

Fast and slow zombies will combine forces to take the castle expeditiously and with as little loss of "life" as possible. Fast zombies will force human inhabitants to begin fighting before they have had time to prepare all defenses. Slow zombies will descend on the castle like an indomitable wave. While fast zombies keep the humans busy at the castle walls, slow zombies will have time to discover openings in the bottom of the moat that lead to the castle's sewer system. (Gross, right?) Pursuing this option, slow zombies will crawl through the grates and "suddenly appear" inside the castle behind the human defenders. These defenders will panic and may open the castle gates. And that's when it really gets good.

Surrounding a remote Arctic (or Antarctic) research station

Fast zombies will just overrun the research facility. Although they may have some initial success overtaking humans unlucky enough to be standing on the outer perimeter of the encampment, the general commotion caused by the attack will alert most of the scientists, who will all pile into the modern, multinational research station. Then it's just a matter of getting on the satellite phone and calling in the air strike. (Probably, some sort of ice storm will make it extra hairy for the humans, but eventually, fighter jets from Chile will arrive and start launching missiles.)

Slow zombies will probably arrive frozen into an ice shelf that is unearthed through some kind of ill-advised scientific research. (Maybe the zombies are the zombies of ancient Antarctic cavemen, or something, which will make them all the more terrifying.) At first, the scientists will take some of these "spontaneously animating specimens" into the mobile lab for testing in a futile attempt to find "the locus of their apparent aggression." And with more and more zombies unfreezing by the minute, the scientists will soon have their hands full. Too full. Probably, yeah, some lucky scientists— like ones with long-range snowmobiles or sailing ships—are going to escape, but lots of humans are going to get confused and run out onto the tundra, where they'll eventually become frozen humansicles that some lucky slow zombie will get to enjoy at a later date.

Fast and slow zombies will utterly fluster and unnerve the isolated scientists by the very fact that they are unclassifiable and varied. (Scientists, unlike most people, attempt to "understand what is happening" and to learn "why animated corpses are attacking everybody." These cerebral projects will prove not only out of place in a time of crisis and mortal peril, but also bedevilingly frustrating as both strains of zombie attack concurrently. An attempt at "sampling" the qualities of the descending horde will yield data that is all over the place, if not out-and-out contradictory. "These moving corpses walk slowly." "Oh wait, they run quickly." "They hardly seem coordinated enough to move." "Now they're jumping and leaping about like athletes.") Needless to say, while these eggheads are stroking their goatees and making declamations like "fascinating" and "remarkable" and "I bet researching these things could get me an assistant professorship somewhere other than fucking Antarctica," the zombies are going to be ripping the puzzled scientists right out of their parkas and lab coats (and no, Thinsulate is not good protection against a zombie).

Encroaching on visiting early nineteenth-century missionaries on a small island off the Haitian coast

Slow zombies are going to have the advantage of appearing to pose less of a threat. The visitors may, at first, mistake these zombies for unwell persons requiring some kind of medical assistance or theological intervention. They may debark in hope of somehow "helping" the sun-stunned "natives" who are wandering around the island and gibbering distractedly. These slow-moving zombies may even be brought onboard for some kind of medical examination. Of course, the well-intentioned missionaries will learn too late that these are not godless, unwashed pagans, but animated corpses who cannot be redeemed (spiritually or otherwise) and whose sole, all-consuming focus is to eat the brains of the living. Probably, at least some of the missionaries will get back to their ship in time to get away, but at least one zombie is going to stow away and then wreak havoc when they get back on the high seas.

Fast zombies will probably seem like some kind of hostile indigenous peoples as yet undiscovered by Westerners. Our intrepid explorers may attempt a cursory communication with the zombies, but the moment the first brain gets eaten by these "vile, heathen cannibals," the missionaries are going to forget all about their religion-spreading project and just light out. Some of the faster zombies may be able to pursue the ship a few yards out to sea (fighting sharks as necessary), but most of the humans are going to get away safely.

Fast and slow zombies are going to lull the visitors into a false sense of security, and then close on them—from all sides—in a carnival of mayhem and slaughter. Slow zombies will seem "intriguing" to the visitors, who will anchor their boat and investigate. That's when you cue the fast zombies to come rushing out of the undergrowth. These fast zombies will overrun the humans and chase them back to their boat, and the slow zombies will follow along and "mop up" humans who get knocked down or chased into a cave or inlet. All in all, it will be a total zombie victory. (Also: number of missionary conversions = zero.)

You see, both fast and slow zombies can get the job done in their own ways, but when combined, they create a multifaceted fighting force that truly leverages its diversity. Whether you find yourself commanding actual slow and fast zombies—or just soldiers who display a variety of times in the hundred-yard dash—count yourself blessed by the advantages this variety will afford you when you attack your enemies.

Note: It is worth pointing out that many artifices of war (caltrops, barbed wire, distracting pornographic murals) are aimed at slowing an enemy down. A great thing about zombies is that, even if you slow down a fast zombie, you've **still got a slow zombie.** And a slow zombie can **still totally eat your brain!**

"Hugging" Your Enemy

Another important tactic that must be employed by any Zombie Commander is "hugging the line." Zombies do this naturally, but, as military history evinces, human soldiers can also employ the tactic to maximum effectiveness.

During World War II at the Battle of Stalingrad, Russian commander Lieutenant General Vasily Chuikov (who, like Ambrose Burnside and Sima Yi, may well have been a zombie himself) was charged with defending the city against a German army with middling infantry but vastly superior artillery and air support. What did Chuikov do? He stayed **right next to** the enemy and never stopped attacking. Just like a zombie.

There was a method to his madness. (Possibly an undead method.) You see, the German fighting style up to that point

had been to first engage the enemy with infantry and then to pull the infantry back and hit the enemy position hard with artillery and bombs dropped from airplanes. Up until that point in the war, this technique had worked just fine.

Chuikov realized, however, that he could effectively negate the artillery and air (which were providing the German advantage) if he always kept his own troops *so* close to the enemy infantry that their positions would be more or less indistinguishable. It was Chuikov who coined the term "hugging" for what he was doing to the Germans. (What you could also call it is: "Cutting them off from their support and killing them.") The technique worked for many bloody months, and the Germans were defeated.

This "hugging" technique has many things in common with the way zombies like to fight. Having no support of their own (except for other zombies), the walking dead do not disengage from an enemy once hostilities have commenced. (As noted, a zombie only stops fighting when it is "killed" or when your brain is in its mouth.) Zombies charge directly into combat. In melee situations, zombies intermix with their human opponents quickly, creating a mass of combatants, in which, from any distance, is difficult to distinguish friend from foe.

Hugging/zombie-attacking your enemy makes it difficult to tell where the "front line" is—or where any line you may have drawn in the sand might be. The zombies are going to be on both sides, doing whatever it takes to come after the enemy.

When you attack your enemy with zombies, their bombardiers and helicopter gunners circling overhead will have a tremendously difficult time deciding where to attack. It will be almost impossible for them to tell where their troops end and yours begin. Same thing for long-distance artillery shells. Your enemy can have the most sophisticated and deadly howitzers on the planet, but will have nowhere to point them when your troops overrun his and turn the battlefield into one giant throbbing bolus of carnage. Your enemy will be forced to sit back and watch his infantry fight yours with no support (and if your troops are zombies, **his will lose**).

Even after your troops have defeated your enemy's infantry, they will **still** be largely immune to any postprandial shelling because they will already be on the move looking for the next target to "hug." (Perhaps the howitzers themselves are next.) They will not pause to rest or celebrate or bestow medals. What Chuikov realized (and what zombies know innately) is that the cardinal sin is to stop for any reason. Be constantly attacking and constantly on the hunt for your foe, and you will negate his long-range weaponry and emerge victorious.

Note: Particularly despicable opponents are liable to just say "fuck it" when fighting zombies and destroy everybody on the battlefield with a bunch of long-range nuclear weapons. However, if the "worst-case" scenario has your enemy **intentionally killing a shitload of his own men**, then, dude, you're doing something right!

29

Think Positive

Nothing's worse than a pessimist, especially in an army. Soldiers who bellyache and complain sow dissent in the ranks and bring down morale for everybody. They create an atmosphere that isn't conducive to fighting effectively. Also, they can be really, really annoying.

Some people are just natural-born complainers: satisfied with nothing, irked by every little thing. It would be impossible to please them, and listening to their inane whines would be a waste of time. But sometimes these "Grumpy Gus" types actually have a point. Yes, they really **are** being asked to march miles and miles with little to no rest. They really **are** being ordered to attack a castle in impenetrable walls and boiling-oil sluices. They really **do** have to kill an enemy soldier and eat his brain if they want something in their stomachs tonight.

If you're going to fight like a zombie or command zombies on the battlefield, you need to divorce yourself quite completely from the notion that you "get" to complain about things. Zombies never complain. They never object to the battle plan as it's been lain out for them (i.e., "Just charge the enemy and eat 'em.") They never campaign for better leadership. (Lucky you.)

This is not to say that they're necessarily positive about everything 100 percent of the time, but zombies at least do what needs to be done without grousing about it. Zombie armies are asked to trudge through caves of self-aware subterranean fungi, endure fire from arrows and catapults, and march directly into row after row of enemy spears.

Zombies just do it. They don't complain. They stay positive. **End of story.**

Some have posited that this complete reluctance to complain might arise from a zombie's general predisposition toward silence, or from a tongue and vocal cords that have long ago rotted away. However, more astute scholars of the walking dead understand that, on a deeper level, zombies realize that complaining would be a bootless endeavor. That's to say, it's not going to change a thing. Zombies were born (in a manner of speaking) to trudge directly at humans, no matter how well armed and armored those humans might be. Zombies understand that often the only way to reach a cadre of these delicious humans is to trudge through hostile environments that range from passively dangerous (quicksand, precarious ledges, avalanches) to actively dangerous (humans with guns, humans with swords, humans with rail guns) to mind-numbingly boring (Iowa). Further, zombies know that there is no **alternative.** If zombies want brains, then a "life" of danger and boredom is the only way to obtain them. Pining after an alternate universe in which brains grow on trees solves nothing. In short, zombies understand the old axiom: "You gotta do what you gotta do." (In a zombie's case, what they've "gotta do" is unleash a holocaust of undead terror and mayhem across the land.)

But a zombie's stalwart tread (into even the most dangerous situations) is indication of more than a lack of pessimism. It is the sign of an individual who has decided to embrace the positive.

If you consider it, zombies "think positive" all the time. Though they are rotting reanimated corpses facing physical restrictions that would daunt and overwhelm the most positive among us, zombies never pause to meditate on what they **can't** do. Rather, they remain focused on what is still possible for them. A one-armed zombie doesn't think: "Damn. One arm. Shit." Instead, he thinks: "I'm gonna find a way to strangle you one-handed, bitch! It might take longer, but hey, I've got all day." A zombie whose torso and legs have rotted into a putrid gelatinous mass doesn't cry over spilled brains about the hundred-yard dashes he will never run. It slithers after humans through sewers and drains, using its natural sliminess to its advantage.

This positivity translates to the battlefield as well.

Slow-moving zombie troops don't think about how much faster the battle would go if they could sprint up to their enemies and start eating them right away. They realize that a battle is like an exquisite ten-course banquet—something to be drawn out and savored for as long as possible. Zombies realize that the battlefield is where they're supposed to be. Killing humans with their bare hands and teeth is what they're supposed to be doing.

So if someone under your command complains or takes a negative view of things, you should probably think about letting him go. He's probably not zombie material.

30

Travel Light, Travel Slow

"An army should forage off the land."
—*Sun Tzu,* The Art of War

From the earliest days of organized combat, soldiers have been weighed down with a bunch of stuff they didn't really need. I'm not just talking about cigarettes, good-luck charms, and letters from loved ones. Soldiers have been required to carry superfluous things like "weapons," "armor," and "food." WTF, right? Seriously, how are you expected to get anywhere when you're saddled with all this stuff bringing you down? Talk about unnecessary.

But don't worry. Zombies are here to help.

Zombies come at you with nothing other than the shirts on their backs (if they are wearing shirts at all), and yet always manage to kick your ass and eat your brains. You've got guns and swords and supplies you've been carrying around this whole time, and yet the zombies still always defeat you. Is this a coincidence? Not at all. Zombies' predilection to "travel light" leaves them able to cross great distances without rush and without rest, helps them adjust to any battlefield combat situation, and motivates them to always be searching for delicious humans.

What's the secret to converting a conventional army into one that travels light and fights like a zombie army? Actually, there are two.

Take it slow.

Forage off the land.

They're not complicated, but they're effective as hell.

Taking it slow is important. Zombies carry nothing with them, but don't use this as an excuse to go running around all the damn time. Zombies remain unhurried. Soldiers who are always marching "on the double" and racing across battlefields to take advantage of things like "cover" are going to expend a lot of calories that will need to be replenished regularly. But zombie soldiers that move at a relaxed, loping saunter (most of them) are going to maneuver a lot more efficiently.

When actual zombies have some humans within sight, the zombies don't usually move quickly to pursue them. And when zombies *don't* have a target, they just meander along absently.

If you want to win battles like zombies do, then **this behavior should be encouraged among your own troops.** If you're just marching from place to place, then whoa, there, pardner. You need to stop and think hard about all of those valuable soldier calories you're wasting.

Lightly encumbered troops moving slowly might sound like the answer to all your problems, but it's only half of it. As noted in a previous chapter, your soldiers are going to be hungry, and you're going to need to reward them with food from time to time. Good food, if at all possible. But also, it should be **the enemy's food** and not your own. The ancient general and author of *The Art of War*, Sun-Tzu, understood this fact, advising generals not to have soldiers bring food along but instead to subsist on plunder and forage whenever possible.

And, when it comes down to it, what is a zombie's "life" if not plunder and forage?

A zombie forages for brains, wherever it is and whatever it is doing. (And it plunders people heads!) Likewise, a successful soldier must be trained to always be on the lookout for his next meal. This will motivate troops to march ever forward (to where new food might be) and never backward (where they have already been and there is no more food).

When training your army, you need to instill the notion that **there is no food except that which you will take for yourselves.** While this might mean that rations could be lean at times, at other times—like when they take a well-stocked enemy position—it will mean a plentiful feast of many delicious excesses.

Your soldiers will be more motivated to charge well-positioned pillboxes, brave a constant rain of arrows and spears, and walk directly into lines of fire if they understand that food and plunder can be the direct result. And as for food, so for supplies.

You need ammunition? Take it from the enemy.

You need blankets and tents? Enemy again.

Flashlights, compasses, and maps? Ditto, my friend.

This policy of plunder will give your troops a very zombie-like lack of attachment to material things. Take what you need whenever you require it. Then when your troops are in a situation where they no longer need cannonballs and tents and GPS devices, they can simply drop them without feeling guilty. Like zombies, your soldiers are not attached to physical things.

They are always "on the hunt," and there will always be more where that (humans) came from.

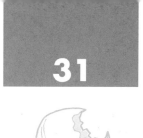

Handle the Truth

Most people can't handle the truth. It's true in that one movie where Jack Nicholson plays a military guy, and it's true in real life. And the truth is, no military force in the history of war has ever been as effective as an army of zombies. Accepting (i.e., "handling") this truth is a vital step to adopting the winning ways of a zombie general.

In war, you face some dire fucking situations. Attack plans can fail utterly. Division after division can be completely decimated by enemy artillery. Your soldiers can show up in this crazy uniform style called "butternut"—which is totally more *tan* than gray—and it's like: "What the fuck are you all thinking with that?"

As a commander, it is unacceptable for you to allow these situations to unnerve you. You must remain clearheaded and cool. You must project an aura of calm. For it is in these situations that your troops will look to you to steel their resolve. You must not let them down. Whatever you're facing, just remember: **Zombies have faced worse!**

So your little counterattack failed, did it? Or your supply convoy got disconnected from the rest of the troops? Or—what's that?—you're in a bunker underneath Berlin and all the news is bad?

Never fear. Zombies have faced tougher situations and "lived" to tell the tale.

Zombies have charged—wave after wave—into moats filled with flaming acid that have decimated them and yet still have not stopped them from attacking. Zombies have lurched into combat against government shock troops in bite-proof body armor, fully aware that their teeth would not be able to pierce these Kevlar bodysuits, yet never short of alacrity to attack. Zombie battalions have sustained direct howitzer hits—reducing their number from four hundred to fewer than ten—and still the survivors have shuffled forward toward their prey.

Zombies accept the lousy situation, then continue on. **That is why they kick ass.**

Zombies have faced every sort of human foe imaginable, from phalanxed hoplites with zombie-proof shields (who screamed something about "Ares" while stabbing away), to line after line of eighteenth-century muskets, to "smart bombs" guided by lasers and satellite imaging. Yet no zombie has ever had to deceive itself into believing its chances for success ("brains") were any greater than they actually were. Even if the information about their position on the battlefield, relative firepower compared to the enemy, and overall chances of success are lousy, a zombie will process it all without hesitation or fear. And then it will keep moving.

Many human leaders have shown evidence of a zombie's indefatigable fighting spirit in the darkest of situations.

Think about George Washington at Valley Forge. He took a bunch of poorly fed, skin-and-bone, half-naked (gee, that sounds like zombies, doesn't it?) soldiers who seemed to be facing certain defeat at the hands of the British, and simply by **not giving up** began to fashion the tools of a victory for the Continental army.

Anthony McAuliffe at Bastogne is another great example. (He might have told the Nazis: "Nuts!" instead of "Brains!" but I think, here, the basic sentiment involved can be fairly called equivalent.) The American troops might have been surrounded by Germans with little hope of a timely rescue, but McAuliffe wasn't about to just give up. He wanted to see what would happen if he didn't. (As it turned out, he was rescued and the

Allies went on to win the Battle of the Bulge.) The point is, even when surrounded, outgunned, and facing a very difficult situation, surrender was never on the table. He knew the situation was terrible, accepted it, and fought on.

If you want to command and lead like a zombie, then never sugarcoat the situation for yourself or your troops. If you've trained your soldiers appropriately, then they should be able to function in any scenario, no matter how desperate or dire.

Remember, the only thing worse than being in a bad situation is being in a bad situation and not having the balls to accept it.

Zombie Soldiers

What are the qualities that a general looks for in his troops? Let's do a little list. Any modern military leader obviously desires soldiers who:

- Will work for free
- Require little or no training
- Enlist for life
- Eschew completely any attempt to think for themselves
- Inspire fear and trembling in the enemy
- Are, themselves, afraid of nothing
- Require very little upkeep and can usually find everything they need by foraging
- Are willing to charge selflessly into situations where imminent destruction is a near-certainty

- Have a complete lack of interest in whether the cause for which they are fighting is "just" or "right" or "unsanctioned"

You can see where I'm going here. These qualities and inclinations—*all* of them—are found innately in zombies.

At this point, we've covered the advantages of fighting like a zombie and the tactical tips involved in leading like a zombie on the battlefield. You've seen how a zombie soldier fights (and seen that it's awesome) and we've covered some of the strategies of the zombie tactician that can allow you to raze your enemies' cities (even as you raise hell on earth).

On board so far? Excellent.

But the dream of conquering continents, becoming an all-powerful undead dictator, and seeing your foes flee before you in cowardly terror isn't going to happen by itself. You're going to have to assemble a fighting force to do your bidding. This chapter will cover the major steps involved in this process.

If you have access to powers that can **actually** raise the dead, it will certainly help things out a lot. People in this category might include:

- Voodoo priests (or at least researchers who've synthesized the zombie-creating powder used by voodoo priests)

- Magic Users level 34 or higher who have mastered all Raise Dead spells and are of lawful evil alignment

- Funeral directors who've been lucky enough to save some of the mysterious glowing goo they found in the asteroid that landed on their property that one time

- Scientists who've been shunned by the mainstream establishment for conducting experiments into the reanimation of necrotic tissue

- Industrialists overseeing large toxic-chemical facilities who have seen fit to circumvent EPA standards by stashing hazardous waste in graveyards (I mean, who's gonna ever know, right? And plus, who's it hurting? The dead people? Ha! [Takes long, fitful draw on Davidoff])

- Socially isolated teenagers who found a copy of the *Necronomicon* in that occult bookstore over on Milwaukee Avenue

(**Note:** Those with the power to create actual zombies will be able to skip ahead to the end of this chapter.) But what if you're **not** a voodoo priest, magic user, or smug factory owner richly deserving of comeuppance? What if you're just some guy or gal who bought this book?

Fear not, for the purpose of this tome is to allow **anyone** to kick ass with the efficacy (and style) of the undead. To that end, this chapter will brief you on how an aspiring leader like yourself—in possession of **no** supernatural or scientific access to creating zombies—can nonetheless muster a fighting force composed of humans, but which will fight (and win) like zombies.

Suffice to say, not everybody who couldn't get into college or just got a girl pregnant will qualify for your zombie army. Your recruiting poster (perhaps featuring a rotting Uncle Sam with half its face missing and one bony digit extended toward the onlooker) may read "I want YOU," but the "YOU" in that sentence will need to be an individual with very specialized qualifications. Zombie recruiting is a careful business, and it's important to understand how it **differs** from traditional recruiting.

Throughout history, armies have recruited soldiers through a variety of methods. The ancient Romans paid soldiers well, offered them large tracts of land in the countries they helped conquer, and provided pensions after they had completed an enlistment cycle. Beginning in the 1600s the British often obtained soldiers through "impressment," a policy of simply selecting people at random and forcing them to become soldiers. Other, subsequent empires have tried different—some would call them opposite—approaches, recruiting the "worst of the worst" and allowing military enlistment to substitute for a prison sentence, deportation, or other censure. Modern first world countries tend to have all-volunteer armies, and so must induce individuals (with a plethora of other options) to decide that the best one for them is to become a soldier.

If you find yourself constructing your zombie army during wartime, there will likely already be conscription policies in place in your country. Likewise, if you are operating under a dictatorship or (just as good) are part of a military junta, there should be no problems, either. Many countries that simply "feel threatened" have required military service as a regular fact of life. If you find yourself starting in one of these situations, thank your lucky headstones and then skip ahead to the next chapter.

If, however, you have the misfortune to be starting a zombie army in a "democracy," where people don't have to do things just because, like, you say so, then you're going to have to launch a recruiting campaign to enlist members in your unholy army of the night. Though it requires an extra step, this is no cause for despair. In fact, it will allow you to ensure from the start that the men and women joining your fighting force are made from the right stuff (which is to say: stuff that is close to decomposing animated corpses that only want to chew on human brains).

In most democracies, those lining up for military service can typically include:

- People from rural areas with no employment prospects
- People from urban areas with no employment prospects

- People with skills that cannot be monetized in the private sector
- People who seek adventure or escape or just want to kill people
- People who are "patriotic" and/or seeking to "serve their country" (I know, right?)

Though these might seem to be limited parameters, this recruiting pool should leave you with a plentiful crop from which to select only the best candidates for zombie soldiery.

You want soldiers who:

- Are naturally and exceedingly inclined toward violence
- Relish hand-to-hand (or brain-to-mouth) combat (though formal martial arts training is not a requirement)
- Can take orders when necessary, but are able to function autonomously
- Are comfortable handling a variety of unusual situations (haunting graveyards, invading centers of commerce, disrupting social gatherings in remote locales)
- Have a "can-do" attitude (especially when it comes to "doing" things to the enemy)
- Are content to be rewarded with food

Don't worry about finding candidates who meet **all** of these qualifications at first pass. The trick is getting as many potential recruits as possible interested in joining up. (Later, you can sort out who the brain-eating elite will be.)

Why do people enlist? Hey, why does anybody do anything? **Remember:** Just as actual zombies can arise in a number of ways, zombie soldiers can come from a variety of backgrounds.

Nuclear waste or industrial pollution can seep into a community and turn the dead *and* the living into completely awesome, murderous zombies. Aliens or a meteorite can land on Earth and deposit some heretofore unknown (and totally kickass) chemical that turns people into zombies. A Harry Potter–type wizard can wave his wand and reanimate the dead into walking corpses. A tourist visiting Port-au-Prince can wander into the voodoo part of town and find out what zombie fans (and Paul Farmer) already know—that Haiti is the rockingest place on Earth! Zombies can arise from all these situations, and more. The point is, they're still **all** zombies.

Your zombie recruits may be tall, short, fat, thin, smart, dumb—it doesn't really matter. When it comes to physical manifestations, you need to have an open mind about what your zombie soldiers are going to look like. Variety is to be **encouraged.** Just as an army of actual zombies must accept the rotting cannibal corpse, the dead-eyed voodoo servant, and the virus-driven sprinter, so must an army of human zombie soldiers accept all manner of mutation, variants, and origin stories.

The important thing is for you—as a Zombie Commander—to embrace diversity. When someone wants to join the military, it doesn't matter if they're white, black, yellow, red, or brown. They say that when someone wants to join the military, the only color that matters is green. (Green for their uniforms, not green for money. [They will be paid very little.]) When someone expresses an interest in joining your army of zombies, the central qualification should not involve their outward appearance, but, instead, an inner desire to fight and kill like a member of the undead.

Other than verifying that an enlistee is not a wanted criminal (and even then . . . ehh), most military recruitment processes begin with a physical examination. You'll want to include your own, of course, with special attention given to the attributes of a good **zombie soldier.** For example:

- Potential soldiers who cannot run, jump, or walk without limping should not be immediately disqualified.
- Blindness and deafness (partial or complete) should likewise not be criteria for dismissal.
- Minimum number of limbs reduced from four to two (though in special cases, exceptions may be made even to this [Maybe somebody is really good at slithering]).
- Visible afflictions likely to strike fear into the heart of an enemy (open sores, infections, evidences of communicable disease) are acceptable, and even encouraged.
- Sexual orientation is no longer a factor in military eligibility. Zombies have no sexual orientation, or sexual functions, at all.

- The inability to read, write, or speak should not disqualify a candidate. (Actually, the quieter they are, the better.)
- No minimum or maximum enlistment age. Zombies can be thousands of years old, and still quite effective on the battlefield. Alternately, some of the most disturbing (to the enemy) zombies come in the form of reanimated kids.

While a traditional general likes to imagine the soldiers under his command looking good in military parade dress, a Zombie Commander understands that soldiers should strike fear in the heart of an enemy (or anyone else) through a show of their slavish devotion to the cause of battle. An opposing solider who sees an advancing column of troops in immaculate uniforms and perfect physical shape will chafe at the bit to muddy and bloody those uniforms and blow them limb from limb. But an opposing soldier confronted with zombie troops **who are already missing limbs** and **who already show signs of physical deterioration** thinks to himself: "Jesus. . . and they're *still* coming?"

Indeed, my friend, they are.

Another consideration is brains. Namely, how they overthink things and prompt people to ask stupid questions. When a group of zombies is laying siege to a remote farmhouse, they don't stop to ask if what they're doing is "for a good cause" or "the right thing to do" or if it "furthers the liberation of the people." No. The mission is to eat some brains, and that's all

Courage is being scared but doing it anyway.

Idiocy is not being scared of zombies and/or attacking zombies. (It's like, dude, what are you even thinking?)

they know. That's all they **need** to know. Being smart shouldn't automatically disqualify someone from enlisting in your zombie army, but if it manifests in their asking questions every five minutes, then, yeah, maybe this is not the best army for them. If a recruit seems overly preoccupied with what your army will be "fighting for" or if the word "why" tends to pop up as you lay out impending "police actions" that you are likely to be a part of, then it's probably a good idea to let that person go. (It doesn't mean he's a bad soldier necessarily, just that he isn't "zombie material.")

Also, you want troops who are excited to fight for you. Zombie Commanders save time by not spending hours writing and delivering rousing, Patton-esque speeches in front of giant-ass flags to their troops. This is because **zombie troops are already roused.** There is no need to convince a troop of zombies that this latest battle will liberate oppressed people, restore land that historically belonged to their people, to further the growth of democracy (or Communism, or Zoroastrianism, or whatever). Zombie soldiers are just happy to be there fighting. They relish the chance to gnaw on some heads.

Most importantly, zombie soldiers need—like actual zombies—to never, ever, ever, ever surrender or flee. **Ever.** This is vital. Make certain that the soldiers you recruit lack the ability to notice it when a battle is going badly, the perspective to see that an enemy force appears overwhelming compared to your own, or any instinct to live to fight another day. For a zombie soldier, there is no day other than today, and there is nothing it would rather be doing than fighting. Zombies will fight for an army that is about to be overwhelmed and is outnumbered ten to one. The zombies don't care. **They just want to fight.**

Indoctrinating Your Zombie Troops

The most important thing about zombie fighting tactics is the way that they will flummox the enemy by defying his expectations. As we've already seen, your enemies expect that a soldier will move or take cover when he sees a gun pointed directly at him. They expect that he will circumvent areas covered with barbed wire or flaming oil. They expect that he will retreat if his side is obviously outnumbered or sustains massive losses. **A zombie soldier does none of these things.** Thus, zombie soldiers confuse their enemies because they don't act the way they're "supposed to." A confused enemy hesitates. In that moment of hesitation, he is killed by zombie soldiers. Repeat this again and again and again—and *boom!*—you've just won a battle, son. **Won it like a zombie!**

On a macro level, opposing commanders like to imagine they know "truths of the battlefield." Truths like:

Flanking an enemy battalion will cause them to rout.

No army continues an assault after it has lost more than fifty percent of its soldiers.

Cut off an enemy battalion from command, and it will cease to function effectively.

Soldiers need, like, guns and swords and stuff.

By instilling the convention-defying fighting tactics of zombies in your soldiers (and in yourself) you will become well-versed in winning through surprise.

"Surprise!"

It's a word pregnant with meanings in military contexts. Usually, one thinks of "surprising" an enemy as involving operations behind enemy lines, such as the appearance of troops in an unexpected situation or a midnight raid on an ammo bunker. Zombie soldiers (and actual zombies) do these things, but they also use surprise by behaving in surprising ways. Whether or not you're commanding actual zombies or zombie-like troops, you can harness these fighting tactics in ways that create effective battlefield results. Your enemies will be surprised by how you fight, and you may be surprised by the results you see.

Once you've assembled your zombie army through whatever recruiting methods you see fit (subsidizing college scholarships, providing pensions, hypnotism, and voodoo power), you're going to want to have an official **Indoctrination Meeting** with all your soldiers to tell them about the surprising fighting styles they're going to learn. If you've built a giant, continent-conquering army, then you probably need some closed-circuit video equipment to show your message to all your troops. If you've just got a smaller army—suitable for conquering the neighboring kingdom—then you can just have them assemble in an amphitheater or something.

First and foremost, you must tell your zombie soldiers that a change is under way. Many of your troops will have prior military experience. Some of them may be lifelong mercenaries with more battlefield experience even than you. Whether grizzled veteran or pale neophyte, let your soldiers know they are about to experience a considerable paradigm shift from any fighting style or battlefield tactics they may have known previously.

Tell your troops that a soldier who thinks he "knows how to fight" will end up dead and useless if he tries to use his traditional tactics as part of a unit that is fighting like zombies. He will seek cover, fail to move forward toward the enemy at all times, and carry way, way more equipment than he actually needs. These divergences from the zombie troops around him will make him stick out and mark him as an easy death at the hands of the enemy. While the rest of the army will be confounding the enemy with actions that appear to make no sense, the traditional soldier will be refreshingly predictable. "Oh, finally," the enemy will say, "something I **understand!**" (The enemy will then level his M-16, flaming arrow, or trebuchet at this "understood" soldier, and utterly destroy him.) Stress to all of your soldiers that they need to behave in this new manner if they wish to survive and win battles. It must be a coordinated effort.

Zombies are all about conformity. A different zombie is a dead zombie. **Only by assimilating into the group will they truly harness the strength of the undead.**

Use this **Indoctrination Meeting** as an opportunity to expound on some of these differences between zombie soldiering and traditional soldiering. If any of the assembled don't feel like these new, zombie tactics are something they can do, then the door's right there. They can walk through it (like a human) instead of sticking around to shamble through it later, toward zombie excellence.

In the past, your soldiers may have been instructed to:

Take cover from enemy fire.

Employ misdirection when advancing toward an enemy.

Wear camouflage.

Carry food and supplies wherever they go.

Retreat and/or wait for resupply when ammunition is exhausted.

Generally, avoid areas the enemy may have seen fit to augment with barbed-wire fencing, moats, land mines, acid pits, or machine-gun pillboxes.

Make clear to your recruits that their new modus operandi will involve acting like a zombie and all that this entails. While—as you know well, as a Zombie Commander—there are a deceptively complex set of rules associated with appropriate zombie behaviors, the central precept for your soldiers may be summed up as:

Always just march directly at the enemy and attack them

It is at this point in your **Indoctrination Meeting** that an unsettling wave of audible skepticism may ripple through your audience. A few may head for the door (enlistment papers be damned!). More will likely voice concern that your proposed fighting style would be "suicide" or "insane" or, at the very least, "a really stupid idea."

When you're faced with a hostile audience that you want to win over, the most important thing is to establish commonalities between yourself and this audience. Hey, you both get up in the morning and put on your pants one leg at a time. You both want success on the battlefield. You both want to win battles with the least possible loss of life (at least for your own troops). You both want to become known far and wide as the greatest and most feared fighting force on earth. Right? Good. I'm glad we can all agree.

Next, tell the story of how you came to have your position as an expert on the total awesomeness of zombie fighting styles, however contrary it may be to their own. Begin at the beginning. Tell the story of how you, perhaps much like them, were once merely a soldier in the lower rungs of the military-industrial complex who dreamed of one day razing continents and bending nations to your will. Then you started noticing how the one fighting force that **always** won battles (and **always** found a way to overthrow even the most entrenched regimes) wasn't composed of humans at all. . . it was composed of the decomposing reanimated corpses of the walking dead. You noticed how zombies could defeat enemies who were more numerous, held greater tactical advantages, and possessed superior firepower (where zombies often had **no firepower at all**). And you thought: "Zombies are cool and all, but why should *they* get to have all the fun?" And so you undertook and extensive study of the precise tactics and practices that allowed them to enjoy this consistent battlefield success. (Or rather, I did, and you just bought this book. But no reason to tell your soldiers that, right?) And you want to use these zombie fighting tactics to create the most effective army in the world. (Or human army, that is.)

Make clear to your soldiers that they have two options. They can leave because this project "seems weird" and "involves zombies." Or, they can get in on the ground floor of something new, exciting, and powerful. They can be part of a movement that's going to change military history forever. They can join a fighting force that is as feared and respected as it is utterly unique (except for, you know, actual zombies).

Continue by expounding on the benefits of membership in an army that fights like a bunch of zombies. They will:

Be encouraged to plunder and rape.

Be feared and respected throughout the land.

Have very little to remember in the way of tactics and techniques.

Win hundred percent of the battles they fight, or die trying. (Maybe don't emphasize the "die trying" so much at first.)

Your soldiers will soon come to revel in their luck at having been selected to be a part of such an exclusive and powerful fighting force. When you help them understand the positive consequences of zombie-style warfare, they will be excited to learn more. Moreover, as they see the extent to which zombie success involves functioning as a cohesive unit, they will begin to self-regulate. They will encourage one another (and discourage bad [un-zombie] behavior).

And once you have your troops on board, **then the slavering and carnage can begin in earnest.**

Always Be Prepared

Okay, first of all, there's a difference between "being prepared" and "undergoing preparation."

Zombies are prepared (all of the time, at every moment of the day or night) to kick your ass and eat your brain. They don't require any prep time to be ready for a battle or engagement. Their fighting effectiveness is not bolstered by a review of the terrain or conditions they will encounter. In this connection, military briefings and mission reports are almost entirely lost on them. They may even attempt to eat the person delivering the briefing.

In this way, zombies exist in stark contrast to the rather ponderous machinations of the modern political and military establishments. Formal conflicts between nations tend to have

several stages, each of which allows conventional generals to prepare their troops for combat. These stages can include:

An inciting event (terrorist attack, trade embargo, failure of a diplomat to notice another diplomat's new haircut).

An internal political debate over the efficacy of declaring war.

A declaration of war.

An attempt to create public sentiment in favor of the impending military action.

A phase of military recruiting.

A phase of military training.

The deployment of forces to contested region.

The actual engagement of the enemy.

There are other steps, too. These are just the main ones.

Because there are so many stages between the inciting event and the start of any actual fighting, armies usually have at least a few months to train their soldiers in preparation for the battles to come. Unlike a traditional soldier, a zombie soldier is literally ready to fight at a moment's notice. A zombie is trained from the moment it slithers out of a graveyard on the hunt for human flesh. Further, zombies never "get soft" if they find themselves away from the fighting for extended periods. They can be idle for long periods with absolutely no effect on their battlefield acumen.

If you want to be the most successful military leader possible, you need to convince those in power that keeping a standing zombie army is the only acceptable military strategy for them to pursue. If you have actual zombies, great—just keep them fenced in in a big valley or something, and unleash them whenever conflict raises its head. If you have human troops who fight like zombies, you'll need to keep them sharp and ready to kick ass at all times. If you find yourself in the employ of a dictator with dreams of world conquest, then this problem solves itself. (Just always be attacking your neighbors.) If, however, you have the misfortune to be a Zombie Commander in a democracy that fancies itself capable of fighting wars "only when threatened," you're going to have to make a little effort to ensure your zombie troops are always prepared for war.

Stage mock battles that allow your soldiers to practice Always Just Marching Straight Ahead. Erect fortifications with giant guns and cannons pointed at your troops so they can practice not flinching in front of them and not taking cover. Create obstacle courses with easily circumvented pits and trenches, and make sure your soldiers just march directly through them. Instigate policies castigating soldiers who are caught moving too quickly. Keep rations low, and tell your soldiers things like: "Gee, I sure wish there was a war on. That way, you could eat as much as you could plunder from the enemies we would constantly be defeating."

An army of zombies during peacetime is a garden that must constantly be tended. (Otherwise, it will become weedy and decidedly un-zombie-like.) However, doing so will have enormous rewards. When war **is** finally declared (and it **always** is), the nations hostile to you will be racing to recruit and train an "effective" fighting force of conventional soldiers to bolster their regular military. You, on the other hand, will have an **awesome zombie army** ready to go. And while your foes are still picking a design for their recruiting posters, you will simply release your zombie army on their land and wait for the inevitable result. (**Hint:** It's victory.)

Leading Your Zombie
Troops into Battle
(Just don't, okay?)

As recently as the early twentieth century, commanders led their troops into battle personally, often standing at the front of the formation and armed with little more than a dress sword.

Then, sometime around World War I, military leaders seemed to reach a collective consensus that this was completely goddamn asinine, and wisely relegated themselves to command centers at the aft of the action. (It was still essential that some form of order be kept on the battlefield, so "squad leaders" were created to lead the enlisted men immediately around them.) These commanders huddling at the back of the battlefields—with their radio equipment, computer readouts, and satellite operations imaging—have only just discovered what Zombie

Commanders have always known: **To command an army, one does not need to physically be part of it.**

Don't believe what you may have seen in the movies. Effective leaders do **not** need to be physically present in order to help their soldiers win the day. Some of the best general-ing has been conducted from comfy armchairs next to warm, toasty fireplaces. Whether you're commanding an army of actual zombies, or just an army of human troops who fight like zombies, you're going to want to do one thing above all when it comes time for actual combat: **stay the fuck out of their way.**

Sending an army of zombies into battle is like unleashing a chemical or biological weapon. It's like setting off dynamite. It's like pushing the red button and choosing the nuclear option. The best thing to do is to unleash them, duck and cover, and hope that the wind is blowing the right way (because zombies are smelly). Your zombies will know what to do, and they will do it until they or your enemy are completely defeated (and possibly eaten).

Getting out in front of a bunch of zombies and attempting to "lead" them (in your little kepi and dress jacket) is just a stupid idea. You're not going to inspire them to fight any better, and you'll probably just make things worse. If you're commanding an army of actual zombies, then the zombies will likely try to eat you. Maybe you could run away from them (toward the enemy or something), but still, if they somehow catch you,

you're just fucked, and then what was the point? If you're a warlock or voodoo priest and you've got some kind of spell on the zombies so they don't attack you, then that's one thing—but you're still just going to be getting in the way. Your presence won't suddenly make zombies want to eat brains any more than they already do.

In the same respect, if you're commanding an army of zombie-like troops (and you've trained them correctly, using the precepts laid out in this book) then they ought to be able to handle themselves just fine without you urging them on like a cheerleader. Just point them toward the enemy and let them charge off on their own. **They'll know what to do.** Your presence would only be a damper on their effectiveness, placing them in potentially awkward situations where they are tempted toward very **un**-zombie-like actions like showing concern for the safety of a superior officer. (If you're dodging cannonballs right and left, your troops might forget their training and get anxious. You don't want them anxious; you want them driven by an insane, atavistic lust to kill the enemy.) Human zombie-like troops may also be confused by your presence and assume it means that you have important information to impart. It's best not to confuse your own troops. (It is hard enough for them trying to live up to being a zombie.)

As noted in the previous chapter, the readiness is all. Keeping your soldiers in zombie fighting shape is a long-term project, not something you can do at the last minute with a rousing speech or by personally leading a charge. When it's the day of the big battle, it's too late to "zombie up" soldiers (be they actual undead or merely undead-inspired). If they aren't already behaving like dynamic battlefield killing machines, no last-minute heroics from you are going to make a damn bit of difference. If, however, you've done things right and planned ahead, then the moment your army notices the enemy **they will instantly attack of their own accord.** When this happens, you can yell, "Charge!!!" if you really want to (but, again, it will simply be a formality on your part).

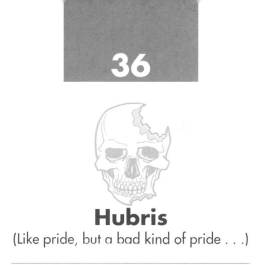

Hubris

(Like pride, but a bad kind of pride . . .)

Every commander of zombie troops or of regular ones faces battlefield situations that challenge his acumen. There will be unexpected developments. There will be acts of God (or Satan, or whatever) that conspire to undo the most carefully laid battlefield plans. There will be betrayals by allies and unforeseen advances perpetrated by your enemies.

No book of military advice (even one about zombies) can tell you exactly what to do in every eventuality. However, there are important precepts that can help you decide what to do when opportunity (for success or for disaster) presents itself. Foremost among these is this:

Pride and arrogance will fucking doom you.

Like, let's say you've created an army of human soldiers who fight like zombies, and you've used the tactics prescribed in this book to kick the asses of every foe who dared to oppose you. But one day you come across an opposing army composed of **actual** zombies. Do you stand a chance against them? It's like, dude, if I have to tell you, then you need to go back and reread this whole book again. **Nothing and nobody can kick ass like a bunch of zombies.** Those who are arrogant enough to believe they can are rewarded with a grisly death at the hands of zombies.

The history of military downfall and failure is the history of hubris—of arrogant pride that denies reality and compromises the most effective of armies.

Napoleon thought that an army that could conquer parts of Europe could somehow therefore conquer a Russian winter. Saddam Hussein thought that if he took Kuwait quickly enough, the matter would be settled and not become a global military issue. That one general-guy in *Return of the Living Dead* thought a tactical nuclear strike against a small Kentucky city would kill all of the zombies (and not just make a lot more of them). What caused these otherwise successful commanders to make such grievous errors of judgment? Pride and arrogance.

I warn you: Even Zombie Commanders are not immune. (In fact, the only things that have ever **reliably undone** an army of zombies are pride and arrogance on the part of their leaders.)

Though commanding an army of zombies is pretty much the sweetest thing ever, don't lose sight of who you are and what you're doing. You are strong, but you are not invulnerable. Neither are zombies.

Okay, this is sort of back to basics, but let's pause to remember that zombies **can** be killed by:

- Being shot (or stabbed) through the head
- Being exploded
- Being completely dissolved in acid
- Being burned down into nothingness by napalm (or a similar accelerant)

Zombies can also be rendered ineffective by:

- Freezing them in ice
- Trapping them in glue
- Removing their teeth and fingernails
- Distracting them with fireworks or fresh brains

Zombies are strong (way more than "Army strong," certainly), but not invulnerable. Zombie Commanders would do well to remember this fact. They can be **undone** by failing to heed it.

In recounting the few instances in which Zombie Commanders **have** been defeated, one sees, again and again, that it is the sin of hubris that causes their enterprises to fail.

Some medieval Zombie Commanders are recorded as having put bronze helmets on zombies and foolhardily considered them invulnerable. These commanders marched their zombies at enemies who trapped the zombies in pits, pushed them into moats, or set them afire. (And here's the interesting thing: If they'd been allowed to continue fighting, the zombies still would have probably won the day, but the Zombie Commander, seeing his "invulnerable" zombies being thus thwarted, ordered a very un-zombie-like retreat.)

The increasingly well-documented Nazi zombies of World War II appear to have been employed largely to augment German infantry by inspiring terror and unease in troops who opposed them. (**Note:** Did German helmets have that weird-ass shape to better protect zombie brains? Get on it, *MHQ*.) However, their effect seems to have been largely negligible, as Nazis were already such bastards anyway that even without zombies the Allies seemed content to use all means at their disposal to defeat them, zombie and human alike.

Both of these examples illustrate important points. Zombies are hard as hell to kill, but they're just not invincible. **If you start thinking they're invincible, you'll lose.** Zombies inspire terror and hatred, but that's redundant if the whole world already feels that way about you. **If you start thinking zombies inspire more terror than they actually do, you'll lose.**

Look, a Zombie Commander has an overwhelming number of things going for him. The advantage is always with the zombie side. No pressure or anything, but if you're leading an army of zombies or zombie-like troops into battle, the only person who can really fuck things up is you. So don't let that happen. Stay reasonable. Keep your perspective. And keep humble (or at least as humble as the leader of a kickass army of the undead can).

Very few enemies have even an outside chance of defeating you. **Just make sure you don't defeat yourself.**

Note: A master Zombie Commander also avoids hubris by keeping alert for the unknown. While remembering what can and can't kill zombies is always at the pinnacle of importance, you also need to be ready for situations that will take you into unexplored territory. I'm not here to tell you into which combat situations you should steer your troops (the Arctic, the bottom of the ocean, outer space somehow). However, I **am** here to remind you that the Tale of the Zombie is still being written. Top scientists are discovering new things about the walking dead every day. As you conduct your undead troops into combat, be prepared to encounter situations in which you'll tread on unknown ground (both literally and figuratively). Each time you guide your zombies into new combat situations, you will learn new things about what can and can't kill zombies. For example, the effects of the following are still largely unknown:

- Electricity
- Elephant tranquilizers
- Black magic
- Radiation (this may actually improve zombies, turning them into superpowerful radioactive zombies—but again, it's unknown)
- Transportation to other dimensions
- Undersea pressure
- Different gravities and atmospheres (usually caustic) found on other planets

And this is not an exhaustive list. Indeed, the range of possibilities is nearly inexhaustible. When your zombies encounter a new environment or a new weapon being used against them, be ready to learn quickly and adjust your battlefield practices accordingly. Don't assume anything about zombies. That's how you get into trouble.

Constantly Invest . . . in a Zombie Army

Whenever advances are made in battlefield technology, zombies will find a way to rise to meet them head-on.

A misconception within the military-industrial complex is that a "technology race" exists among all armed nations, and that all armies must constantly improve and upgrade their equipment and weapons of war for fear of "falling behind." Most experts posit that, in one form or another, this race has always existed. Military historians point to groups of cavemen struggling to craft bigger and better clubs, Bronze Age armorers wrestling to craft a light and lethal mix of copper and tin, and contemporary nations racing to upgrade their computer systems and laser-guided missile technology ahead of their enemies.

While this system has always worked out well for military contractors and defense companies, it can to be largely unnecessary when zombies are introduced into the mix.

Zombies have a way of thwarting military technologies across the spectrum and across time, from the most primitive constructions of ancient man to the most cutting-edge modern technology. Leaders speak of making "investments in technology," but if you want to command the most indefatigable and superior fighting force in the world, you only need to invest in zombies. Once.

No new technology or upgrade to a better weapon has ever allowed soldiers anywhere to effectively defeat zombies. The smartest minds in military technology have been trying—since the beginning of time—to come up with something they can sell that will make human soldiers as effective as zombies. They have always failed. They have failed because they've missed the fact that a zombie's superiority on the battlefield does not derive from its being tantamount to a laser-guided rocket launcher or radar-guided torpedo gun. A zombie's effectiveness derives from **its priorities on the battlefield and its style of fighting**, not from its similarity to a weapon that can be commodified and sold to traditional soldiers (who will just use it to fight in **conventional** wars using **conventional** fighting styles).

Beware the military contractor with its handsome spokesman and the impressive multimedia presentation promising his defense system can give your soldiers "zombie battlefield awareness" or provide them with "firepower equal *or superior to* the effects of an army of zombies."

Blasphemy. Blasphemy and idiocy.

Happiness doesn't come in a pill, and zombie killing power doesn't come in a bomb or a gun. That's life. The real things—the things that matter—aren't things you buy. They have to be earned. Through hard work, perseverance, or possibly some kind of voodoo ceremony in a graveyard in Haiti. But those who would seek to convince you that simply by upgrading a conventional army with some trendy new piece of equipment which will endow it with the killing power of the undead are selling the dream of a fool.

Compare and contrast zombies with the typical military innovations that require constant reinvestment and refinement:

- **Edged weapons**—Can rust, go dull, or break, and constantly require sharpening.
- **Zombies**—Can lose teeth or fingernails, but still retain an ability to murder you.
- **Firearms**—Require ammunition and must frequently be upgraded to new models.
- **Zombies**—Already have all that they require. While "new models" can appear from time to time and join a horde, there is never any need to replace older ones.
- **TNT, Explosives, Mines**—Are only "good" once.

- **Zombies**—Can kill your troops on repeated occasions.
- **Nuclear Bombs, Nuclear Missiles**—Destroy entire cities.
- **Zombies**—Destroy only the populations of entire cities; infrastructure, priceless cultural artifacts, and public works will remain 100 percent intact.

So, like we've covered, make sure you keep your zombie troops well-trained and hungry for brains at all times, but that's the extent of any further investment you need to make after raising an army of zombies. (Really, the only further investment is time.) Advances in technology—though often amusing—are never the concern of a Zombie Commander.

Whatever they invent, **zombies will find a way to foil it.** Whatever they upgrade, **it will still not be deadlier than zombies.**

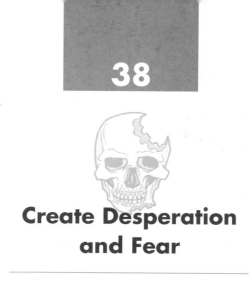

Create Desperation
and Fear

Zombies don't only win military engagements through
force of numbers and combat awesomeness. Zombies win
because their enemies have been reduced to quivering masses
of terrified fruit preserves. No one is immune from the terror
inspired by zombies. Properly trained and attuned, a zombie
army can instill a creeping dread in even the most stalwart of
foes.

Fear is important. **Fear helps you win.** Great generals have
always understood the role that fear plays on the battlefield.

As is well documented, the great Genghis Khan liked to send
Tibetan throat-singers into battle alongside his troops. Though
they provided no additional killing power, the eerie noise they
made struck fear into Khan's opponents who often decided

253

that they were demons. Something as seemingly innocuous as singers helped Khan drive his opponents from the battlefield all the more quickly.

Pop quiz, smart guy. What's the scariest thing in the world? (No, not "zombies." Brownnoser.) The answer is: **the unknown.** The most frightening and troubling thing in the world is that which we cannot identify or classify. Zombies, ghosts, mummies, and yes, even flamboyant, dramatic vampires are unnerving to encounter in combat situations because they combine qualities from both the living and the dead.

Humans look at something and always try to make that first, most primal determination about it: **is it dead, or is it alive?** But here's the thing: it's walking around like something that's alive. It's probably walking toward you and attacking you, actually. It may also be talking, moaning, or even inviting you to a romantic midnight rendezvous on a palatial Southern estate (stupid vampires). And these are **all** things that the living do. But when you look a little closer, you see deathly pale skin.

You see flesh that has rotted away from bone, or become translucent entirely. Maybe you even see a relative who you could have sworn passed away last year. So it seems like it might be dead and also like it might be alive.

There are no atheists in foxholes.

This is largely attributable to their having been eaten by zombies, however, and not to any specific re-evaluation of a theological position.

And when your brain tries to think about something that is **alive and dead at the same time**, it kind of sputters and breaks and suddenly you feel like something is very wrong here. And you become unnerved and **very, very afraid.**

I don't say this to detract from the practical fears one experiences when facing zombies. Those are there, too, and they're nothing to slough off. Being eaten alive, killed with teeth and fingernails, and having one's brain removed from one's head are very reasonable (and very **terrifying**) things to be afraid of. But that fear—that practical fear of being killed in horrible ways—is something that even conventional soldiers can instill. Further, it is something that conventional soldiers have trained themselves to withstand. Throughout military history, soldiers have resigned themselves to dying at the hands of the enemy. They have accepted the fact that they might be captured, tortured, or killed in horrible ways. Training your soldiers to instill this kind of fear, while absolutely necessary, **is not sufficient** for a Zombie Commander. Those who seek to create a fighting force with the effectiveness of the undead must also learn to instill a **deeper, cosmic, more troubling fear** in the battlefield foes they face.

An enemy who cannot classify what he is fighting will become desperate—desperate to know who or what they are, and also desperate to extricate themselves from the situation. No soldier anywhere has ever said: "A battle where I don't know what the fuck I'm getting into? Awesome! Let's do it!" When under attack, knowledge is key. Therefore, you must act in such a way as to withhold as much information as possible from those you engage militarily.

When you attack in the manner of zombies, you create considerable ambiguity. This ambiguity will create fear. This fear will create military victories.

When closing on your enemy, you want to create unknown elements for your enemy. This will create desperation and fear. You want to maximize the number of things he doesn't know about you. Among the things he should "not know" you may include:

- How many of you there are
- Where your forces are
- What your forces look like
- What **exactly** you want from him
- How **exactly** you intend to get it

I emphasize the word "exactly" above because obviously some conditions of your relationship will be apparent from the conditions of your meeting. You two are ranged as foes on a battlefield. You want to win the engagement, and you want your enemy to lose. But what does winning "look like" to you? (A surrender? A retreat? Full-scale desertion?) This should be **your secret.** When your enemy eventually learns that he is fighting zombie soldiers—who only define victory as killing all of the enemy until none are left alive—it will be too late for him to adjust his tactics accordingly.

Attacking like a zombie—eschewing cover and subterfuge—will also spread fear of the unknown in the enemy camp. Your foe will be unable to believe that your entire army is comprised of that giant horde just marching down the middle of the field toward him. He will be unable to allocate his own forces to any degree of satisfaction, and will be constantly second-guessing himself. One common trait of foes facing zombie armies is to "overthink" their own strategies. These generals tend to assume that their enemy's stealth indicates that a guerrilla-style attack will commence shortly, or that his foe is concealing a weakness or lack of firepower. What a surprise it is, then, when the zombie army emerges **right fucking in front of him**, Always Just Marching Straight Ahead, and armed to the teeth (perhaps with actual teeth) Both the potential of how you **might** attack him and the unexpected directness with which you **do** attack him will combine to make your enemy desperate and afraid.

When your enemies are fearful and confused they will make bad decisions. This will make it easier for you to kill them. End of story.

Dealing with "Failure"

There is no general agreement, even among the most astute students of the walking dead, as to whether or not zombies have the capacity to "fail" at something, especially in the sense that you or I might understand the term.

Zombies try to do things (open doors, tunnel upward from subterranean burial mounds, bite through pith helmets) all the time. Sometimes they succeed, and sometimes they do not. Yet a zombie's ultimate goal is always to eat the brain of its enemy. If an action—even one that seems to be a misstep—brings a zombie closer to that goal, one is hard-pressed to call it a "failure."

Zombies are naturally curious creatures. In many cases, their reanimated brains contain little to no trace of the collected

knowledge their bodies had in life. Thus, for a zombie, each action and interaction with something (an automobile, a power line, a flotilla of battleships) presents a new opportunity to learn about the world. I should not give the impression, however, that zombies are interested in "pure science." Zombies are interested in "eating your brains out of your head." They may be fairly called curious in that they are curious about what actions may bring about this desired result. Though certain actions may fail to result in edible humans, there are frequently unexpected and (to a zombie) delightful results.

For example, zombies struggle to understand mechanisms like automatic doors, turnstiles, and elevators. Their interactions with these devices are often frustrating exercises that do not result in the appearance of edible humans. Sometimes though, the unexpected occurs. A zombie that has "failed" to locate delicious humans may accidentally touch a circular plastic button next to a bifurcated metal wall, and find that—moments later—this wall magically opens to reveal a box full of terrified humans with no place to flee (and who seem intent on mashing their own set of buttons to no avail as they scream for help that never comes). A curious zombie may search fruitlessly for humans in a series of shipping crates on a wharf; yet when the zombie is sealed inside one of those crates, transported for several weeks as part of a ship's cargo, then deposited on the docks of a coastal population center, it will find that it has succeeded in locating the presence of humans after all, as soon as that shipping crate is opened by an unlucky merchant. Consider, too, the zombie who explores the basement of a morgue or mortuary—there it will find only dead, embalmed brains (not worth eating). But if the zombie conducts a thorough search of the premises that lasts until dawn, the zombie may yet encounter the mortician arriving to get an early start on his day's work. (The zombie will, likewise, get an early start on eating the mortician's brains.)

The point here is that serendipitous things happen to zombies all the time as a function of their natural curiosity.

When you're commanding zombie troops in battle, you can depend on them to extend this curiosity to the battlefield around them. While they may sometimes depart from the day's battle plan (Always Just Marching Straight Ahead), you can generally count on any short-term failures to result in longer-term successes. If your zombie troops have trouble opening a door, crossing a drawbridge, or stopping an enemy tank, don't automatically assign these events the status of a "failure." Your zombies are simply learning about their opponent, and they will use the lessons they garner—sooner rather than later—to crush and destroy these same foes.

So encourage your troops to be curious and not to fear failure. Remind them that setbacks can often become unexpected steps in the right direction, and every experience (good or ill) provides new information. You don't want a bunch of soldiers who are paralyzed into inaction by a fear of failure. You want them shambling forward into combat with the unconcerned swagger of a zombie.

40

Final Thoughts

When you command an army of zombies, you will win battles. (If you take anything away from this book, I hope it's that.) Zombies are ceaseless hunters. They are intrepid travelers. They are 100 percent dedicated to hunting their enemies, and are willing to risk "life" and limb to do so (assuming they still have limbs). All of these qualities combine to make a horde of zombies the greatest terror one can encounter on the battlefield.

Drill sergeants have tried for years to instill in soldiers the qualities that, to a zombie, come naturally and freely. **Self-assurance. Propensity toward violence. Toughness. The ability to survive in the wild for long periods. Bravery.** With the possible exception of "proclivity to obey orders" there's

nothing an army sergeant can teach a zombie that it doesn't already know.

We've established the multitude of qualities that make zombies the most feared warriors on the battlefield today, and we've also reviewed the ways a zombie army can be recruited, constructed, and set into motion. You've got the tools. You've got the motivation. There's just one question left:

Where do you want to go from here?

Will you be an evil despot necromancer who uses an army of the undead to terrorize the countryside and bend the people to his will; a mad scientist who blends zombies with cyborg technology to creature futuristic supersoldiers with circular saws grafted to their hands and rocket launchers on their shoulders; or will you be a good old-fashioned medieval zombie warlord ushering in a new dark age via your horde of walking skeletons in helmets and chainmail? Perhaps you will use zombies to "fight for your country" or to encourage the cultivation of a particular religious or political ideology. Perhaps—like zombies—you just want to fight because it's a way to get what you want.

Whatever the case, when you use zombies on the battlefield, the possibilities become endless (much like the life of a zombie itself). I hope that much is clear to you. Your troops can cross the uncrossable, withstand the unwithstandable, and do the unthinkable. The only remaining step is to decide what you want them to do.

I've taken you as far as I can.

The rest, my friend, is up to you.